BRUTALIZED

JR THOMPSON

I am; it was wonderful meeting you on our flight. So glad you're back in church!

JR Thompson

This is a work of historical fiction. The storyline was inspired by historical events. Names, places, characters, and specific incidents are either the product of the author's imagination or are used fictitiously, and any resemblance to any actual persons, living or dead, organizations, events or locales is entirely coincidental.

All scripture quotations come from the Authorized King James Version of the Bible.

Cover designed by Lynn Andreozzi.

Manuscript edited by Beverly Cooper.

ISBN# 978-1-7337673-6-1

I am dedicating this book to my nephew,
Marshall Thompson, whom I pray the Lord will
use to accomplish mighty things.

FOREWORD

When I first caught wind of the Irish slave trade, I was in shock. I couldn't believe I had graduated from high school without ever hearing such a thing existed. A few quick, simple searches online nearly had me believing it was all a fairytale. However, when I took the time to do some thorough digging, I was stunned at what I found.

I wrote *Brutalized* after reading *The Irish Slaves* by Rhetta Akamatsu, *Bound With An Iron Chain* by Anthony Vaver, *White Gold* by Giles Milton, and *They Were White and They Were Slaves* by Michael A. Hoffman II. I also received inspiration from many online sources.

Brutalized is based on historical events, but the characters and specific incidents come straight from my imagination.

I intentionally used modern language throughout this book to make it easier to read while retaining much of the terminology that would have been used during the colonial era.

CONTENTS

CHAPTER ONE

TAKEN CAPTIVE

The horrifying events unfolding during the wee hours of Friday, May 14, 1632, would haunt twelve-year-old Callum McCarthy for the rest of his days. With the sun not yet rising above the Wicklow Mountains, unimaginable fear engulfed the lad. Never before had the boy woken to a sweat-flavored palm mashing against his chapped lips.

Callum's baby-blue eyes sprung open. Crouching over him was what appeared to be a madman with oily, dirty-blonde hair and an unkempt beard. The man's flaring nostrils and rapid, heavy breathing made him look more monstrous than human. The man's hair and eyes told Callum he wasn't from Dublin. The young boy would have studied him further, but before he had a chance, the madman whisked him from his wooden-floor-sleeping-space into the chilly night air.

Already weak from malnutrition, the preteen could do nothing to prevent the stranger from dragging and locking him into a fully-enclosed horse-drawn cart.

Slowly, the heavy breather uncovered Callum's mouth while holding one finger over his own lips. With a stern expression, the man tilted his head to the side, straightened it, and tilted it a second time.

Understanding the gesture, the lad scooted tight against an older teenager held fast in stocks and chains. Callum didn't recognize the young man. Then again, the teen's face was mostly hidden behind layers of dirt and fresh, smeared blood. Between that and the darkness, even if the two had been best friends, Callum wouldn't have been able to identify him at first glance.

Callum's eyes widened as his captor removed an iron collar from the wall. Shaking his head and squinting, he gritted his yellowish, plaque-coated teeth. If only there were a way to wake himself up from this brutal nightmare!

That's what it was; it had to be. Nightmare or not, the madman clamped the frigid, heavy collar around the lad's neck.

Not wishing to see anything more, Callum shut his eyes as tight as he could, inadvertently sending his ears into hyper-alert mode. Shuffling feet and clanging chains, sniffling, and more shuffling feet ushered in a moment of eerie silence.

A pair of calloused hands grabbed the lad's bare feet. Callum flinched but didn't struggle against the man who hoisted his legs a few inches off the floor. An ice-cold chain brushed against Callum's shin, but only long enough to send pulsing shivers down his spine. The boy slightly opened his eyes just in time to see his feet securely fastened into stocks. The madman gave the chains a fierce yank.

The door flung open. A second rogue, even more repulsive in appearance than the first, literally threw Callum's nine-year-old brother, Aedan, into the cart. Aedan yelped as his head banged against another kid's knee. The madman seized Aedan by the throat, "Not another peep or I'll pop your head off. That goes for the whole mess of ya!"

The only other time Callum could remember seeing such horror on Aedan's face was that day when he had fallen through the seat of the outhouse. Callum smirked as he remembered hearing Aedan screaming, "Somebody help!" He recalled hustling to the outhouse, where he found Aedan's hands gripping the top of the seat for dear life as his bodyweight nearly dragged him into that putrid-smelling pit of human excrement. Yes, that same look that had donned his brother's face nearly a year before had reappeared.

With circumstances growing more dire by the second, Callum imagined himself putting on the strength and courage of a warrior — breaking his brother, the other hostages, and himself free from bondage.

Why couldn't he turn that dream into a reality? Taking a deep breath, Callum jerked forward with every ounce of strength he could muster. Unforgiving, the collar around his neck choked him half-to-death. The lad coughed several times, and water puddled in his lower eyelids. The brute was securing Aedan in chains, and Callum was powerless to stop him.

With Callum's older brother, two younger sisters, and parents still in the house, the ordeal was far from over. Surely somebody would bite an attacker's arm, punch one in the throat, something! If even one relative could get the upper hand, freedom might become attainable, if only for a moment.

The next time the door opened, Callum saw his four-year-old sister, Boann, kicking and screaming. That's when the lad got angry. He had a closer bond with Boann than with any of his other siblings. Oh, how often he had rocked and sung her to sleep! How many times he had kissed her boo-boos! Callum was more like a second father than a big brother to the girl. It was his job to protect her. If only he could grab her outstretched arms and rescue her from danger! A tear of helplessness trickled down the boy's cheek. Oh, how badly he wanted to do something!

Not long after Boann was bound, a rogue brought seven-year-old Glenna in. The girl's eyebrows were lowered and drawn together, forming a 'V' just above the ridge of her nose. Her eyes were narrow, and it appeared as though daggers would shoot out of them at any second. The man was holding her tighter than he had the others. The deep scratch on his nose probably had something to do with that. At least somebody in the family had thought fast enough to put up a fight. Too bad she hadn't poked an eye out!

There was still hope. So far, Callum hadn't seen his parents or his fourteen-year-old brother, Sullivan. Surely an entire household couldn't be taken down in one night by a small pack of foreigners.

The door whipped open again. Sure enough, the people-thieves had Sullivan, and he was in no position to escape. One man held his feet, and another had his arms wrapped around Sullivan's chest. Callum shook his head. Unless his parents intervened, he and his siblings were in grave danger.

Callum peered around the dark cart, certain a few of the children from his neighborhood had been kidnapped as well. With practically no lighting, he couldn't make out any of their faces. Like him, the others in the cart were too afraid to speak. The only sound to be heard was that of heavy footsteps just outside the cart.

A few minutes passed, but the McCarthy children's parents never came, bound or otherwise. Soon the cart bounced furiously along the dirt streets. The ride was torture as every bump caused the shackles to scrape Callum's ankles. Blood oozed its way from the wounds down both feet onto the floor beneath him. Others whined and complained about their increased pain as well.

Callum did the same for a little while before recognizing his own selfishness. "Glenna, did you see Father and Mother before they brought you out?" he asked.

With her bottom lip jutted out, Glenna shook her head.

"Did anybody see or hear them?" Callum asked.

Callum's siblings and most of the kids in the cart were far too scared to speak. Shaking heads was the best the lad could get out of them. There was no way the adult McCarthys had slept through so many kidnappings. Callum feared his parents had suffered a fate worse than his own.

After ten minutes of silent fear, Sullivan whispered, "I think I recognized one of them."

"One of the kidnappers?" Callum asked.

"Did you get a look at the man who was missing an eyebrow?"

Callum nodded.

"I'm not one-hundred percent sure, but I think he's either kin to or a friend of Darcy's. I've never seen him up close before, but a man with a similar build has talked to Darcy several times during the past few months."

"Where?" Callum asked.

"Different places, but always when they are off by themselves."

"Any more of that jabbering," a brute hollered, "and you'll lose your fat little tongues!"

The man's warning was an effective deterrent. The talking stopped. Unfortunately, the silence got Callum's mind reeling. If Sullivan was right, and the lad hoped he wasn't, one of the brutes had somehow earned the trust of a family friend. On second thought, if that were the case, why didn't Darcy ever talk about him? Maybe the man was harassing her somehow? Either way, Darcy was in considerable danger.

For well over an hour, the cart continued bouncing along cobblestone streets before skidding to an abrupt halt. Callum had mixed emotions — he was relieved to stop hitting bumps, terrified more families would be targeted, hoped someone would rescue him and the others, and greatly feared he was nigh unto death.

Alarming heavy footsteps tromped toward the back of the cart. A lock was fiddled with for a few seconds before the door swung open. A wicked middle-aged hair-deprived man chuckled, "Cry all ya want to now! Nobody 'round here cares what's happenin' to ya!"

The money-loving brute unchained Glenna from the others and picked her up, collar still in place. The fearless seven-year-old attempted to shove the villain away from her, "Get away from me you fat, bald-headed tyrant!"

The man laughed while toting Glenna through a dark doorway. It sounded like he rushed her down a flight of stairs. If only Glenna were older and stronger so she could put a hurting on that brute!

Callum wished he could find a way to harness Sullivan's strength and Glenna's courage. The only way to escape this atrocity was to fight. Callum thought hard. He couldn't do anything about his strength, but he could think himself into having enough courage to stand up for himself and his family. He had to fight back, even if it cost him his life. It wasn't like going with the flow would guarantee his safety anyway.

By the time one of the vermin got to Callum, the lad had himself psyched up. He slugged the unsuspecting ogre on his double-chin.

The man grinned, stretched his broad hand across Callum's face, held it for a second, and slammed his head against the wall without warning.

Callum's body went limp, and the man wasted no time sliding him across the cart and through the door.

Once outside, however, Callum proved he had only pretended to be unconscious. Elbowing the kidnapper between the legs, he bellowed out a futile panic-stricken, "Help!" at the top of his lungs. Surely someone would hear and run to his aid as he had to Aedan's in the outhouse.

As if hearing nothing, the madman jerked Callum up, tossed him over his shoulder like a sack of potatoes, and toted him down the steps into a room containing little to no light. He dropped Callum to the ground, and another man grabbed the collar on his neck and chained him to a steel bar running the length of the room.

Shouts of "We're not animals" and "Let us go" rang out among many of the captives.

Others strove to quiet them down by yelling things like, "Do you really think they're going to listen to you?" or "Shut up so we can hear what's going on."

Callum didn't care who said what. He and his siblings were in danger, and his parents had possibly been murdered. One way or another, he would escape his low-life captors and check on his father and mother — even if he had to take out that entire group of kidnapping thugs first! But how could a scrawny boy of twelve possibly undergo such a feat? How wasn't important. Callum could do anything if he set his mind to it.

First things first, that chain had to come off. Yanking on it with every ounce of his might did nothing more than scratch the lad's wrists worse than they had before. Breaking free from that bar was about as likely a possibility as catching twin baby gnats with worn-out chopsticks. There had to be another way. Perhaps he could pull one over on them. Yes, indeed, that would work! It had to!

Wrenching his body around frantically, Callum loudly unloaded a train full of gibberish. For a good five minutes, he flailed, tearing a layer of skin from his neck, ankles, and wrists. He grunted and groaned in pain.

"Enough!" A captor hollered. "No more drama!"

Ignoring the man's demands, Callum tugged and jerked at his chains as if he had gone mad.

The barbarian grabbed a tuft of hair on the back of the twelve-year-old's head and forced him to look toward the ceiling. "I'm not stupid, lad." The man pulled out a jackknife and held it to Callum's throat. "Cut out the fake seizure routine before I cut out your Adam's apple!"

Defeated, Callum bit his tongue and stilled his body. One wrong move and future generations would remember the lad as The Headless Preteen From Ireland.

"Wise decision," the ogre growled.

Callum wasn't so sure. What if the man was bluffing? Had he kept up the act, he may have earned a chance to break the guy's nose. But it was too late for that. After a brief stare-out, the kidnapper moved on.

Fighting back his tears, Callum breathed a sigh of relief. He was safe, for now anyway. The lad closed his eyes. Things would worsen before there was even the slightest chance of them improving. Perhaps he'd have been better off if the man had just slit his throat and gotten it over with.

A teenage girl whispered to Callum in a soft, scared voice, "Ya must be dumber than a pinecone. Ya nearly got your brain splattered."

"What did you expect me to do? Sit here while they starve me and my brothers and sisters to death?"

The girl peered into the distance for a moment. "Ya think ya could boost 'em to safety if they pile a bunch of dirt and rocks on top of ya?"

"And allowing these brutes to keep me tied down like some kind of demonic maniac is helping them?" Callum scoffed.

"Nah," the girl whispered, "but ya have to wait for the right timin'."

"I suppose that's what you're doing?"

"Ya! Sooner or later, those smelly chums are bound to move us outta here — when that happens, ya can help me beat 'em senseless. They started this war, and we can't let 'em win it!"

Half-smiling, the lad said, "I like the way you think. My name's Callum, by the way. What's yours?"

"Pleasure to meet ya, Callum," The girl whispered. "I'm Ryanne."

Callum's smile widened. Ryanne was a classy name. It seemed fitting for someone like her — athletic build, wavy shoulder-length blonde hair, and a voice that spoke of both intellect and kindness. But it was far from the time or place to waste time on such vain thoughts. "How do you know they're going to move us?" he asked.

"That's what slave traders do, Pinecone. I'm gonna start calling ya that. Ya don't mind, do ya?"

Her words hit Callum like a ton of cobblestones. Ryanne was right; he should have known. For months, people had warned of slave traders working the area. A brute had snatched him in his sleep and planned on selling him to people of an unknown land. How had he not put two and two together?

He could not allow that to happen. Not to him. Not to his siblings. And not to the sweet girl chained next to him. Somehow, they would escape. They had to. But how? Ryanne said they needed to wait for the right timing. But from what Callum had seen so far, the longer they waited, the worse things got.

Suddenly it dawned on him. How had Callum forgotten? "My uncle!" he exclaimed.

"Ya uncle? Ya think he has somethin' to do with this?"

Callum nodded, "When people started coming up missing, Uncle Keir set off on a one-man mission to stop the traders. He'll find us."

Ryanne slightly tilted her head and pulled her mouth to the right for a few seconds. Instead of maintaining eye contact, her eyes shifted toward the ceiling, "Ya sure about that one, Pinecone? Nobody's been talkin' about such a brave act. How long ago would ya say your uncle began his mission?"

Callum folded his lips in, making them disappear for a moment. After several seconds of silence, he said, "I don't know. About a month ago, maybe. You didn't hear about a man rescuing a bunch of kids from a building like this one?"

Ryanne shook her head. "Sorry, Pinecone. Can't say I did."

"Uncle Keir killed a whole army of slavers all by himself."

"And ya think he's comin' for us now, do ya?" Ryanne asked.

Before answering, Callum's mind wandered back to that last night when he had seen Uncle Keir. The lad was returning from the outhouse when he heard loud voices pouring out of his family's living room. "Get out, and don't ever step another foot on my property!" his father had yelled just before Uncle Keir stormed past Callum.

Confused, Callum went inside to find his parents glaring at one another. "What's going on?" the lad asked.

"It's none of your concern," his father scolded. "What went on here today is never to be spoken of again. Got it?"

It had been six years since the fight, and Callum still didn't know what it was about. The only updates he ever got on Uncle Keir's whereabouts came from Darcy. According to her, Uncle Keir was on a mission to stop poor Irish from being stripped out of the country.

"Pinecone?" Ryanne asked.

The lad jumped. "Sorry about that. I thought I heard somebody coming. What were you saying?"

"How sure are ya that your uncle's comin' for us?"

"How sure am I?" Callum repeated. "I'm positive we'll be out of here in no time. Can I ask you a question now?"

"Ask away, Pinecone!"

"Why do you talk so differently than everybody else?"

Ryanne giggled, "That's why!"

"What do you mean?" Callum asked.

"I'm different on purpose. Having two older sisters, an identical twin, and three younger sisters who all have my face, hair, and build, I was tired of blending in."

"So you made up your own accent?"

"You're smarter than I thought, Pinecone."

Callum looked around the room. "I don't see anybody here who looks like you. Where are your sisters?"

"Home," Ryanne said. "They were sleepin' when I slipped out the window."

"Your family doesn't know you left the house, and now you've been kidnapped?"

Ryanne smiled sheepishly, "Maybe you're not the only one as dumb as a pinecone."

"Why did you sneak out?"

"To meet up with a couple of friends," Ryanne said. "But they never showed."

CHAPTER TWO

BOARDING THE AUSTERE

Even though Callum's nightgown was the same kind every impoverished child in his neighborhood wore, uncomfortable calamanco, the sentimental value of his had made it impossible to part with. Unlike everything else Callum wore, his older brother hadn't first outgrown his sleepwear. Nor was it made from a tattered piece of material a neighbor had thrown out for the garbage.

For several months after Callum's birth, his mother suffered from a mental breakdown and her neighbor, Darcy, volunteered to be the lad's nurse. Even though the lady treated all of the McCarthy children well, Callum was her favorite, and everybody knew it.

For Callum's ninth birthday, Darcy measured him and knitted the nightgown he was still wearing on the night of the kidnapping. He never grew tired of that thing. At home, he put it on each night just before nesting amongst his siblings on the floor beneath a shared blanket. But now, the gown that had brought him so much comfort somehow felt less than adequate. Chained to a steel bar in a bone-chilling room with no cover and no way of snuggling against a brother or a sister, Callum was shivering. Until that very moment, he hadn't realized how thin that calamanco had gotten over the years.

Most of his peers had somehow managed to fall asleep, and those still awake were beginning to nod off as well. For the first time, Callum noticed how the other soon-to-be slaves were dressed. Some were fully clothed, some were in nightclothes, others were only clad in underwear, and at least one had no covering at all. Perhaps Callum's thin, outgrown nightgown shouldn't be complained about after all.

Loud, hurried heavy footsteps thudded down the stairs. Oh, how Callum hoped it was Uncle Keir coming to his rescue! Hopefully, he had freed Mr. and Mrs. McCarthy before coming for the kids. Better still, perhaps they had patched up their differences and were working together as a team. Convinced that was so, Callum couldn't keep the grin off his face. In no time, the door to their temporary prison burst open and the dungeon filled with nearly one dozen burly men — but Uncle Keir nor Callum's parents were among them.

Callum tensed. Those foreigners were up to no good. Every single one wore the same stern expression on his face. They were men on a mission and probably not the type who would take kindly to resistance.

The ruffians spread out. The one missing an eyebrow stopped before Sullivan and grumbled something Callum couldn't quite make out. His older brother nodded calmly. The brute unchained the teen, grabbed him by the arm, and forced him to his feet. Oh, how badly Callum hoped Sullivan would put up a fight! If any of the McCarthy children stood a chance of gaining a victory over the brutish men who had kidnapped them, it was Sullivan. Most everyone in the neighborhood referred to him as Sully The Bully. Rarely a month went by that somebody didn't stop by the McCarthy house complaining to their parents about who Sullivan had beaten up. He was their best hope.

Callum quietly watched with anticipation. His brother attempted to free himself from the ogre but was no match for someone more than twice his size. With mockingly dark laughter, the captor wrestled Sullivan into the stairwell and out of sight. Three seconds later, a series of thuds, grunts, and groans brought Callum a sense of both hope and fear. Before long, things grew quiet. The struggle was over. More than anything, Callum wanted Sullivan to barge through the door without his captor. Several minutes after things quieted down, the door opened, but it wasn't Sullivan who came through it. It was the brute, and he was alone.

"What did you do to my brother?" Callum shouted.

As if he hadn't heard a word, the ruffian made his way toward another group of captives. If Sullivan were dead, Callum would find a way to repay evil with evil. He might not be able to kill that man, but he could poke his eyes out!

One at a time, more captives were unloosed from bondage and escorted away. Every time a man returned to the room, Callum feared he would be next. Not knowing what was happening outside those doors was terrifying. For all he knew, his peers were being brutally tortured.

A rough-looking shirtless man with a mustache that hid his upper lip grabbed Callum's arm and began unchaining him in anything but a gentle fashion. It was the opportunity the twelve-year-old had been waiting for, the moment when he would find out if he had what it took. Could he free himself and his siblings from a band of hardened criminals?

For once in his life, Callum didn't wimp out. Stomping the kidnapper's toe, the lad simultaneously head-butted the man in the ribs before attempting to run for his life. Tripping, he fell flat on his face. What a stupid move! The man he had just assaulted kicked him in the side. "You might live to regret that decision," he said, lifting the preteen off the ground, flipping him upside down, and toting him out of the room that way. Instead of covering his body, Callum's nightgown now covered his face, making it impossible to see anything. He cried out in pain as his head repeatedly hit the floor beneath him.

The ogre laughed, "Serves you right," he muttered.

At the top of the steps, an unfamiliar voice met them. "Another rough one, heh?"

Callum wished he could see the barbarian's face, but his nightgown was still covering his head.

"Attempted an escape," the man with the overgrown mustache said.

"Ship it to the colonies. If it survives the voyage, it'll lose that rebellious spirit or it'll lose its blood."

It? Callum was a *he*, not an *it*. But it wasn't the time or the place to sweat the small details.

The brute handed Callum off to another man, who tossed him into a cart and hastily chained him to other captives. Callum scanned the faces around him. None of his siblings had been placed in the same cart. He looked around a second time, hoping to catch sight of Ryanne; she wasn't there either.

Sleep-deprived, hungry, thirsty, and in excruciating pain, the last thing Callum wanted to do was hear a bunch of fussing and fighting. Not that he had any way of shutting it out.

"We're only here 'cause you talked me into sneakin' out with you last night," one of the other captives argued.

"You're the one who attracted their attention by smashin' the bottles!"

"Don't forget who tripped over his own two feet when those monsters were chasin' us! We'd have been out of there had you not been cryin' about twistin' your ankle."

On and on, the blame game went. Callum was confident they would have knocked each other's teeth out if it weren't for their being bound. If nothing else, the lads' squabble showed him how he and his siblings sounded when they fought day in and day out. Had Callum been secured next to Sullivan, they'd have undoubtedly fought as well. After all, being the oldest, Sullivan should have done a better job of keeping an eye out for the rest of them. With talk of slave traders in the area, the oldest should have been sleeping by the entrance.

Eventually, the cart slowed to a halt, and the argument subsided.

Being closest to the door, Callum was the first to be approached. One of the rogues fumbled with his chains. Where was Uncle Keir? If he were still alive, he had to act fast, or it would be too late for a rescue.

Callum couldn't take any chances on waiting for his uncle. As soon as the lad's hands were loose, he swung a fist and hit the ogre's chin. Unphased, the man dragged Callum out of the cart.

As Callum's feet landed on the cobblestones, he stopped squirming to take in his surroundings. Three ships, more enormous than anything Callum had ever seen, blocked much of the ocean view in front of him. At least, he had to assume that was an ocean he was looking at. The deep blue water stretched as far as the eye could see. Everywhere Callum looked onshore, carts were unloading passengers, many but not all of which were teenagers and young adults.

Callum's eyes shifted from cart to cart, hoping to catch a glimpse of Uncle Keir, his parents, his siblings, or the pretty girl with the classy name. They had to be there somewhere. But there were so many carts. So many captors. So many people running this way and that. The chances of spotting anyone he knew were slim.

With all the hustle and bustle about him, Callum failed to notice the giant of a man storming in his direction. That is until the giant stopped dead in front of the lad and glared at him as if he had done something terribly wrong. Callum couldn't help but notice the man's piercing, deep brown eyes or the scar on his right cheek.

After letting out a distasteful grunt, the man pulled one of Callum's captors to the side and spoke roughly with him for a moment. Upon his return, the man held up a ferocious-looking whip that made Callum cringe, "Turn up those ears, red-legs! The name is Sir Nicolas Sadler, and I am the shipmaster of *The Austere*."

Red-legs was a term unfamiliar to Callum, but it didn't take a rocket scientist to understand he was referring to Callum and all of the other poor Irish who had been taken captive.

Callum eyed the shipmaster's whip for a moment before studying his face. He was taken back by the man's jerky, cold, dark-colored eyes that screamed of evil. That whip-yielding, one-eyebrowed master of the ship wouldn't hesitate to beat or kill anyone on his ship. Callum knew it would be a foolish move to rebel. He could only hope for a short voyage.

"Anxious buyers are awaiting you in the colonies," Sir Nicolas Sadler went on. "I will not tolerate insubordination aboard my ship. Twill be a long, uncomfortable, and dangerous passage. Follow instructions, and you will receive fair treatment. Ignore or defy them, and my crew will handle you like the pathetic animals you are."

Many silent heads nodded. But a young girl with plaited hair blurted out, "I want to go home!"

Sir Nicolas Sadler motioned for the sickly-looking girl to approach him. With the collar still on her neck, and her bony wrists chained together, the girl hesitantly made her way to him. Her quivering lips and pleading eyes made Callum want to jump in to help her, even though he knew that wasn't possible. Callum wouldn't have wanted to be in that little girl's sandals for anything.

"Perhaps I failed to make myself clear about insubordination aboard *The Austere!*" the shipmaster's face reddened. "You no longer have a home or family! For the next seven weeks, you belong to me! You'll do *what* I say *when* I say!"

Sir Nicolas Sadler was unmoved by the tears streaming down the little girl's face. Turning his gaze to one of his crew members, he said, "This red-leg gets nothing to eat or drink for forty-eight hours. Make it happen!"

Returning his gaze to the group, he thundered, "We've wasted enough time here! Slavers, load the cargo!"

Callum swallowed a lump in his throat at the realization that Uncle Keir wasn't going to perform a last-minute rescue operation after all. Worse, Callum was the first one standing in line. The lad had never before boarded a ship, been enslaved, or been referred to as a red-leg. Sure, he had heard of the colonies, but he had no idea what that far away land might be like, although he convinced himself that life there couldn't be too much worse than the one he had been living in Dublin.

With Callum's father being a drunkard and his mother an emotional basket case, neighbors constantly accused the McCarthy family of theft. There was never enough food to go around. Most of Callum's and his siblings' clothes were worn out. Perhaps, as unlikely as it seemed, this could turn into a good thing. The new family he was going to live with was probably rich. If so, there would be plenty of food to go around and he was certain they would give him some nice new clothes. He willingly walked down the pier and boarded *The Austere*.

After ascending a long ramp, the crew directed Callum and the rest of the young people from his cart onto the ship before one of them barked commands at a dark-haired teenager standing a few feet away, "Jacob!"

The young man, whom Callum guessed was no older than fifteen, stood perfectly still, with his back unnaturally erect. He raised one open hand to just above his brow. Even though Callum had never seen a salute of any kind, he understood Jacob's actions as an outward display of submission to the older crew member.

"Jacob! Red-legs to the cargo hold!"

"Yes, sir," Jacob said, rushing over and grabbing the nape of Callum's neck. Callum didn't understand the need for such harsh treatment. Never had someone so close to his own age handled him in such a manner. Jacob pushed him along the deck and eventually into a stairwell.

Once they were away from the adult slavers, Callum attempted to start a conversation with him, "You don't look much older than I am."

Jacob shoved Callum, causing the lad to tumble down the stairs.

Callum lay there for a second, in more pain than he knew possible, yet thankful to be alive.

"That fat mouth stays closed unless directed otherwise, red-leg," Jacob ordered. "On your feet!"

Callum attempted to push himself up, but the pain was overwhelming. He groaned.

"NOW!" Jacob shouted.

Callum looked at him through a set of squinted eyes.

Jacob grabbed the lad's ear and forced him to his feet. "Move it!"

As slowly as Jacob would allow him to go, Callum limped across the floor, peering through the darkness into an anything but empty cargo hold. There were far too many enslaved folks to count. They ranged from five or six years of age up into their mid to late twenties. Each one was lying down and chained to the person on either side of them.

Several yards down the aisle, Jacob stopped. "Climb up on this shelf. Lay on your back. Your feet need to be on this end."

Callum could have figured that one out on his own since it was the position everyone in the cargo hold seemed to be in. Instead of saying so, he complied in silence.

Jacob chained Callum to the others. The lad grimaced as the power-wielding teen secured the chains on his ankles.

"Too tight?" Jacob asked.

"A little."

The teenager laughed. "Good," he said while using both hands to pull the chains much tighter than they had been before.

Callum sucked in a deep breath, feeling as though his feet were ready to pop off his ankles like an exploding pimple. Instinctively, he tried to reach for them, but the chains made such a move impossible.

"Jacob!" a gruff voice hollered from the upper deck.

"On my way, sir!" Jacob shouted back. Lowering his voice, he said, "The first one to move becomes food for the sea monsters!"

Jacob sprinted toward the stairs. Once he was gone, Callum nervously turned his head to look at the young man lying on his right. "You're not from Dublin, are you?"

The young man spoke harshly in a language unfamiliar to Callum. He switched his attention to the young lad on his left. Unfortunately, as soon as Callum's eyes met with the youngster's, the boy turned to face the other direction.

A horrendous stench filled Callum's nostrils. The mixture of body odor, urine, feces, and rotten flesh was nearly unbearable. It took everything Callum had to keep from vomiting. If he had to spend the next seven weeks unable to move while breathing in such atrocious smells, he feared survival might not be possible.

Jacob returned before Callum had much time to think on such things. "Quit dragging your feet!" he shouted, escorting a group of captives through the hold. "Climb up there, lay on your back, feet toward me," he ordered.

One of the captives, about sixteen or seventeen years old, stopped dead in his tracks and got nose-to-nose with Jacob. "You're pushing the wrong fella. Do you know—"

Jacob punched the stout young man in the mouth before he could finish his sentence. Whoever that slave was, he knew how to brawl. Sounds of scuffling, grunting, and groaning filled the cargo hold before Sir Nicolas Sadler charged in.

Within seconds, the commotion between Jacob and the slave was over, but the master of the ship was furious. "Bring that poor-white earth scratching scum to the main deck. Make an example out of him! And Jacob, he won't be the only one setting an example if you allow another red-leg to get the upper hand on you. I did your grandmother a favor by allowing you to join me on these voyages, and I expect you to earn your keep."

"Yes, sir. Sorry, sir," Jacob said, immediately gripping the angry slave's arms.

"Wait, Jacob," the master of the ship said. "Do you remember your grandmother's words as you boarded this ship for the first time?"

"Yes, sir," Jacob said.

"Repeat them back to me."

Jacob's face reddened. Lowering his voice to that just barely above a whisper, he said, "What you need, Jacob, is a man with a firm hand to beat the naughtiness out of you. Mr. Sadler, I give you my blessing to be as rough on this boy as you need to be. I will not allow him to live with me until he learns how to be a gentleman and to put in an honest day's work."

"You know my mother and your grandmother were life-long friends. I will not let your grandmother down by not bringing you back as a changed young man. This is your final warning, Jacob. As you punish this rebellious piece of scum, keep in mind you're only a step away from receiving the same punishment from me. Now get this poor-white up to the main deck!"

Callum felt terrible for the young man who had stood his ground. He hoped he wasn't about to receive a dose of that whip, but deep inside, he knew that's what was about to happen. He even felt a bit of compassion for Jacob, now that he knew the lad wasn't in his position by choice.

The entire ship grew silent — no more hustle or bustle, no more slaves brought into the hold. But the eerie stillness didn't last long. The sound of a whip making its first cut into a slave's flesh brought a long, drawn-out yelp of excruciating pain echoing through the hold. Jacob may have been only fourteen or fifteen, but it sounded like he swung that whip with the strength of a grown man. Callum shuddered as the whip cracked a second time. That first yelp paled in comparison to the horrific scream the second lash brought. As the lashes and pain-filled shrieks continued, the slavers overhead got rowdy. Hands were clapping. Feet were stomping. It sounded as though the spectators were amused by the older teen's punishment.

After twelve torturous lashes, Jacob escorted the slave back to his place on the shelf. In a gruffer voice than before, he said, "Get up there, and this time keep that mouth closed!"

CHAPTER THREE

FEEDING SEA MONSTERS

There's nothing quite like having dead bodies dragged past you, especially when those doing the dragging are so merry about their work. "The monsters of the sea are gonna be doin' some fine dinin' today," one of the crew members remarked with a smirk.

The body of the young lady they were lugging was swollen to nearly twice its normal size. Her corpse smelled like a mixture of rotten eggs, stinky cheese, and dozens of dead rats. Callum's stomach churned. It was the fourth body that slid past him in the two weeks since he had boarded *The Austere* — three he believed had died from illness, and one from a severe beating.

Callum continuously shook his feet, hoping to rattle his shackles loud enough to drown out the sound of the corpse scooting across the floor and banging its way up the stairs. Some things are easier to deal with the more you experience them; this was not one of those things.

"More food for the fishes!" one of the crew members shouted as her body reached the upper deck. Squinting his eyes, Callum stuck his tongue out, hoping not to hurl. If only there were a way to plug his ears! The lad longed to return to Dublin. Even if his parents had been whisked away by the barbarians, he could probably live with Darcy. He and his siblings had stayed with her many times in the past. Then again, if Sullivan was right about Darcy's private talks with one of the people-thieves, the chances she was still alive and retained her freedom were slim to none.

If going back to Dublin weren't an option, Callum would even be okay with arriving at the colonies to begin his new life there. He wasn't hard to please. Anything would be better than spending another day aboard *The Austere*.

A sharp elbow jabbing into Callum's right side brought that thought train to a screeching halt. The young man next to him didn't speak English but certainly knew how to communicate. Callum tried to inch away from him as best as possible — that was hard to do with only eighteen inches of sleeping space. As much as Callum wanted to return the elbow, he knew it would result in another elbow-to-rib fight, and he had already partaken in plenty of those. He hopped half an inch to his left — it was the best he could do.

From the other end of the cargo hold rang the voice of another captive who had a talent for making up his own songs. Callum could listen to him sing all day long:

As this ship continues to sail
We won't lose hope
We will not fail

Folks here keep on dying
We will be strong
And not resort to crying

We're heading to the colonies

At least we have hope
We can stop lying in feces

These slavers like to treat us wrong
Wait 'til they hear
The rest of my song

God's watching every step they take
Judgment is coming
And they'll burn in a fiery lake

He won't let them get away
With hurting little children
And treating them like prey

Callum didn't have to see the bold singer to admire his character. That voice became his inspiration to keep going, to never stop fighting. There was a light at the end of the tunnel. Callum just had to stay alive long enough to find it.

If Darcy had taught the lad anything, it was the importance of maintaining a positive attitude through the darkest of storms. That's not to say Callum always followed that advice, just that she had gotten him to commit it to memory.

The singing stopped as abruptly as it had begun. Less than thirty seconds later, Callum knew why. Jacob had entered the cargo hold, "Alright, red-legs! Half of you are coming off the shelf at a time. There won't be any talking or shoving each other around. You'll do exactly as you're told. Nothing more, nothing less. The smallest act of rebellion will result in an immediate lashing for the offender and cause the entire group to forfeit food and water for seventy-two hours."

The rules were fair — the discipline extreme. But if there was anything to look forward to aboard *The Austere,* it was exercise day. Once a week, whether they needed it or not, all of the captives were taken to the upper deck, worked out, and bathed.

Anxiously Callum listened as chains around him came off, and captive after captive rose to their feet. Nothing sounded more beautiful than chains coming off so many enslaved folks at once.

After fifteen minutes, Jacob finally made his way to Callum. Having his arms and legs free for the first time in at least seven days felt fantastic. Joining the line of other prisoners, he let out a sigh of relief. How amazing it felt to have no one else's sweaty body rubbing up against his!

Once all the kinks were out, Callum pondered what his future might hold. He envisioned himself alongside many others dragging brush or fallen trees beneath a blazing hot sun. In his mind's eye, he imagined a man built something like Sir Nicolas Sadler following him and the others around, cracking a whip in the direction of anyone shirking their duties.

In time, once Callum gained his master's trust, he would run for freedom. Where he would go or how he would find shelter and food, he didn't know. But the lad was confident about one thing; he would not spend the rest of his days serving some wealthy fellow from the colonies without getting paid for it. Ideally, he would find a way to turn the tables. The red-legs would become the slavers, and those affluent folks from the colonies would face the sting of their own whips.

Twenty minutes into his daydreaming, Jacob made the announcement Callum had been waiting for, "Let's go, red-legs!"

Callum couldn't help but grin as the line crept forward. Above, orders were barked at slaves as they entered the upper deck. Callum found himself in a state of envy. Those on deck had it made! They could see the sunlight, feel the breeze, smell the fresh air, and move about. Getting hollered at would be well worth it!

It took a while, but eventually, Callum made his way to the top. "This way, red-legs!" a burly brute shouted.

Using his whip, the man motioned toward the rear of the deck. No words were necessary. Callum's group hastily made their way to the spot their assigned crew member had selected for their calisthenics session.

As soon as all were in place, the burly man with the whip and three other slavers assembled before the prisoners. "Arms above your heads!" the leading crewman shouted. "Fingers pointed toward the sky!"

Just as Callum got his arms in the proper position, the man issued another series of commands. "Touch your toes! Stand up! Do it again! And again! And again!"

The facial expressions and body language of others said they did not appreciate exercise time as much as Callum did. But that was *their* problem.

"Jog in place. Raise those legs higher!"

One of the slavers walked amongst their ranks. Sweeping Callum's feet out from under him, he yelled, "I said raise those legs higher! You can do better than that, red-leg!"

Even that Callum didn't mind. If he had to choose between being handled that way all day, every day, and being chained to a shelf, unable to move while lying in the dark, his choice would have been easy to make.

After a lengthy period of exercise, it was bath time. "You red-legs reek! You smell worse than a pile of whale guts!" The slaver's words might not have been kind, but Callum had to agree. He, for one, couldn't wait to be cleansed of bodily fluids and feces.

One after another, the crew members doused the captives with buckets of seawater. It was cold but refreshing nonetheless.

Chapter Four

SOLD

Unlike many who boarded *The Austere* with him, Callum survived the voyage without becoming food for the sea monsters or having his flesh torn open by a whip.

"Harbor arrival less than an hour away," Sir Nicolas Sadler growled. "Jacob, ready the merchandise for inspection. Start with a dozen of these red-legs. Send 'em to the upper deck to get cleaned up!"

Callum was thankful to be first in the line-up. It never ceased to amaze him how difficult it was to stand after another week of being chained to a shelf. Ever so slowly, the lad stretched his arms out, bent his knees, and straightened them again.

"Alright, red-legs, march!" Jacob shouted, pointing toward the steps.

The teenager didn't have to tell Callum twice. Leading the pack, he hurried toward the upper deck, where he met beautiful rays of sunshine and a not-so-beautiful member of the crew who shouted, "You five, over here!"

"Next group, this way!" another man yelled a few seconds later.

Callum and a few of the guys in line behind him followed the first crew member, a man with a receding hairline and a bulging forehead, for a stroll around the deck. "You bunch of poor-white earth scratching scum! How do you even tolerate yourselves? Not only did you cake yourselves in manure and urine, but you saturated your clothes with vomit!" The man gagged while hurling a bucket of cold water at the group.

"Turn around," the man ordered before dousing them with another bucket of water. "Scrub yourselves clean! Time is of the essence!"

They may not have had any soap, but Callum was determined to get himself as clean as possible. According to Darcy, a person's physical appearance speaks volumes of their character. Callum already felt awkward envisioning a bunch of strangers examining him from head to toe. Being dressed in an embarrassingly stained nightgown didn't help the matter. Callum scrubbed his body and his nightgown with all of his might until the crew member shouted, "Better! Now for some physical activity to speed up the drying process. You," he said, pointing to Callum. "Fill these buckets and return them to me immediately. You're in charge of keeping them full."

Callum scrambled to snatch as many pails as possible before rushing to the side of the ship. At the same time, the crewman continued shouting orders to the other captives, "You there, scrub this section of the deck," "You, polish up these railings," "By the time we get to the harbor, *The Austere* will be sparkling clean," "You, get down there and help him with that floor!"

Continuously filling buckets for four other captives was draining — especially after having so little physical activity in the past seven weeks. Callum survived nearly two months without a formal introduction to that whip, and he sure wasn't going to mess that up now. He had to think about something else. Something positive, perhaps. That shouldn't be too hard to do. Setting down two heavy pails of water, the lad thought about the shelf in the cargo hold. Working on the upper deck was far better than being chained down there! And he was sure whatever work he had to do in his new life overseas would be as well.

Callum's positive thinking didn't last long. As he went for more water, he witnessed a boy who couldn't have been any older than seven on his hands and knees scrubbing the deck. His face was a light shade of green, and he was sobbing like a baby as he worked. Callum would have told the boy to lay down if he were in charge. Perhaps he would have had somebody place a cold rag on his forehead. The poor fellow needed somebody to pat him on the back and assure him everything would be okay. But that's not what he got! Instead, a crewman drew his boot back and gave the lad a cruel kick on the behind, "Quit that fussing, and put some muscle into it, red-leg!"

Callum dropped the empty buckets. There was no excuse for bullying an ill child. Callum may have only been twelve, but if he were to sneak up behind that man and box his ears — oh, it would never work! He would undoubtedly get caught in the act and have his flesh torn. Frustrated, Callum picked the buckets up again and angrily proceeded to the ship's side for refilling. He tried to return to optimistic thinking but couldn't do it. Not when he had to keep walking past that poor lad and the brute who had kicked him. Somehow, Callum would force himself to get the job done without allowing his emotions to take over.

More and more slaves appeared on deck, with each group assigned to their own set of crew members. For forty-five minutes, Callum filled bucket after bucket with water. Finally, sir Nicolas Sadler made the announcement he had been waiting for. "We're pulling into the port. Get these poor-whites lined up, shackles in place, hands secured. Potential buyers will board ship momentarily."

Callum's eyes widened as the land everyone referred to as the colonies came into view. He had only about a second to look before a crew member grabbed his arms and ordered him to hold still. For once, Callum didn't mind having the chains put on. This time it didn't mean he was returning to the shelf. The lad was getting away from *The Austere*, sir Nicolas Sadler, Jacob, and the rest of the crew, and if they had to chain him up for a few minutes during that transitional period, he could handle it.

"Red-legs!" Sir Nicolas Sadler shouted at the top of his lungs. "Turn up your ears. Potential buyers will be boarding *The Austere,* and many of them will thoroughly examine you. I expect your full cooperation. No speaking unless I, one of my slavers, or a potential buyer commands it. Violators will face terrible beatings before being fed to the monsters of the sea."

Callum didn't like that man, but that didn't stop him from complying.

Suddenly, somewhere in the neighborhood of one-hundred fierce-looking men, in addition to a few ladies, boarded the ship. Through the corner of his eye, Callum carefully observed the potential buyers as they made their way along the line of captives. Some inspected every new slave they came to, while others seemed interested in a select few.

Several minutes passed before a man stopped in front of Callum. "Something about your eyes caught my attention," he said. "They're the brightest I've seen among the captives. The smug expression on your face, however, tells me you've got some fight in you."

Callum tensed. Sir Nicolas Sadler's words echoed in his ears. No matter the compliment or the insult, he could not speak unless instructed to do so.

"Let's have a look at these arms," the potential buyer said, gripping the lad just above his elbows. "A bit frail there, lad, but we could work on that. I'm going to give you some thorough consideration."

That man, Callum thought, was probably brought up as if he owned the world. He didn't have an ounce of kindness to his name. At least he was still moving and checking out other potential purchases. Callum did not want to go anywhere with that ogre.

It wasn't two minutes before another fellow stopped by. Unlike the first one, he was the silent type. Walking a complete circle around the twelve-year-old, the man looked him up and down like one might do when trying to decide whether or not something was safe to eat. He too felt the boy's biceps. Letting out a disappointed sigh, he moved on without uttering a word.

Rejection is not something one takes lightly. Callum tried to see himself through the eyes of the man who had been so dissatisfied with him. He was too thin. Too weak. If Callum were looking to purchase a slave, he wouldn't have selected himself either. He would be a waste of money.

Before the lad could continue sulking, a third man stopped. Everything about him was different than the other men. For starters, he was only a fraction of their height. He walked with a cane. With a bit of a stutter, he asked, "Wha... wha... what's your na... na... name, cracker?"

Callum knew better than to mock people, but it was hard to take the potential purchaser seriously. How could someone his size who spoke with such a bad speech impediment be anybody's master? Reminding himself once more of the shipmaster's instructions, he said nothing more than he had to, "My name is Callum, sir."

The man tapped his cane on the ground a couple of times while staring deep into Callum's eyes. "Ha... ha... how old are ya... ya... you, lad?" he stuttered after a moment of awkwardness.

"Twelve."

"That ra... ra... rusty-colored ha... ha... hair of yours. I've sa... sa... seen it before. Most of the time, on young ma... ma.. men who aren't too qu.. qu... quick to submit to a... a... authority."

Struggling not to laugh at the man's persistent stuttering, Callum turned his gaze to other potential purchasers heading in his direction.

"La... la... look me in the eye, cr... cr... cracker," the man demanded, putting his cane beneath the boy's chin and forcing it to rise a bit. "Da... da... did they ha... ha... have to take the wa... wa... whip to you on that ship?"

Callum shook his head, "No, sir."

"You're not la... la... lying to me, are you?"

"No, sir."

Skeptical, the man moved his cane to the bottom of Callum's gown and lifted it to his shoulders. Callum felt his face reddening as the tiny little man looked him over, front and back, for signs he'd been a troublemaker. Not finding any scars, he pulled the cane away, allowing Callum's gown to fall back in place.

The lad's eyes filled with water. He didn't want to cry, but how could he not? He didn't want to go home with any of these men! At the same time, he worried about what might happen to anyone a purchaser didn't select. Would they reboard the ship, be taken to another destination, and forced to parade around in front of more masters and mistresses? Would they become food for the monsters of the sea? Whatever was going to happen, he wished he could get it over with.

As the man walked away in silence, an older woman's loud, clamorous voice suddenly met his ear. "Too fat," she fussed, moving past an older teen.

"Too ornery looking," she said of another.

"Not healthy enough," she grumbled, getting closer to where Callum was standing. She paused in front of him, but only for a second, "Too puny."

After Callum was poked and prodded by another twenty-five people or so, a young couple approached him. "He's a nice-looking lad," a lady said.

"He is, indeed," her husband agreed.

Unlike the others, the couple didn't touch Callum. "Have you ever worked on a plantation?" the man asked.

"No, sir," Callum said.

"Are you a fast learner?"

"Yes, sir."

"My wife and I have only been married for a few months and are in the process of developing our plantation. We want to make sure the first servant we bring to our property is the right fit."

Callum didn't know how to respond to such a statement. Per the shipmaster's instructions, he wasn't supposed to talk unless asked a question anyway. Both the man and his wife had gentle spirits about them. The lad certainly liked these folks better than any of the others who had talked to him. If he had to be purchased by somebody, he certainly hoped it was them.

"Are you a runner?" the wife asked.

"No, ma'am."

Sir Nicolas Sadler clapped his hands a few times, interrupting the young couple's inspection. "Ladies and gentlemen, the auction will now begin." As the couple moved away, Callum's eyes went to Sir Nicolas Sadler, who was pulling another teenager out of line. "Interested parties may now bid on this handsome, robust red-leg. At fourteen years of age, he's got a solid back and many years of good service in him. Let's start the bidding at ten shillings."

"I'll give ten shillings!" a man shouted, raising his hand.

Callum's breathing shallowed. People were buying and selling other human beings before his very eyes. Not only that, but he was up for sale in the first slave auction he had ever seen.

"I'll give fifteen," someone yelled.

"One pound right here!" the first man countered.

A third man joined the bidding war, "One pound and ten shillings!"

The woman who had been so particular jumped in, "I'll give three pounds for the ugly cracker."

The crowd was silent. Callum may have only been a lad, but he knew three pounds wasn't very much money — not for forty or fifty years' worth of labor. Surely someone would bid higher.

"Three pounds going once," Sir Nicolas Sadler said... "Going twice... Sold to the little lady."

That poor teenager! Life at her plantation would certainly be anything but pleasant. Callum hoped the lady was only at the market to buy one slave. One after another, he witnessed well-to-do men and women engage in bidding wars over the best prospects. The master of the ship collected anywhere from ten shillings to five pounds depending on the age, health, and size of the slave he sold.

Eventually, it was Callum's turn. "Next, we'll be accepting bids for a twelve-year-old boy. He's thin and inexperienced but can be a powerful workhorse with proper training and firm discipline. Who'll give me ten shillings for him?"

Callum held his breath. He wasn't too keen on the shipmaster's suggestion that he receive *firm discipline*. It made him sound like a heathen.

The crowd was silent, but only for a couple of seconds. "I'll give five shillings for him," a man shouted. Callum was happy to see it was the last man who'd spoken to him. Out of all of the slaves up for auction, they wanted him. And the feeling was mutual.

"Not yet, partner," Sir Nicolas Sadler replied. "Surely somebody out there is willing to pay ten shillings for the boy?"

Silence. Callum's heart was racing. How he hoped no one else would bid!

"Okay... five shillings then. Going once... going twi—"

Callum breathed a sigh of relief. He was going to go home with the kindest folks in the colonies.

But it wasn't over just yet. "Alright, alright!" A man Callum hadn't seen before interrupted at the last second. "I'll give you seven shillings."

The auctioneer was pleased, "Now we're getting somewhere," he said. "Seven shillings... do I hear eight?"

There was that dreadful silence again.

"Seven shillings... going once... going twice... sold to the tall gentleman there in the back."

Callum's thoughts and emotions went ballistic. A stranger had bought him. No one was going to ship him off for another auction. He wasn't going to become food for the monsters of the sea. He was the property of a planter he knew nothing about — a slave with no rights, no freedom, and no family.

CHAPTER FIVE

FIRST NIGHT AT THE GILLCREST'S

Imaginations are funny things. The mental picture Callum had of where he was headed and the reality of where he ended up couldn't have been more different. His new master, Josiah Gillcrest, had a large plantation. That part matched up with what he had envisioned. But the property dwellings weren't at all fancy. The shack Callum was assigned to was more run-down than the dump he called home in Dublin.

Nervously, Callum looked up at the planter, who was towering over him in the doorway of his new home. "You're afraid of me," Master Josiah laughed. "A healthy fear of your master will do you well. If it keeps you following orders and prevents you from attempting to run off, you won't have anything to worry about."

Callum's stomach was in knots. How was he supposed to feel about this stranger? No one would ever get kidnapped out of their homes and sold away from their families if it weren't for people like that man who was now, whether intentionally or unintentionally, making the lad feel anything but comfortable. It took him a moment to find polite words to say. Words that might prevent him from getting onto his master's naughty list. "I won't give you any trouble, sir," he said.

Master Josiah smiled. For the first time, Callum realized the man was missing one of his front teeth. He tried not to stare.

"It was giving me a lot of pain, and I had my son yank it out," Master Josiah said. "Now you can quit your wondering. You haven't had any supper this evening, I presume?"

Rubbing his belly, Callum shook his head again and said, "No, sir."

"I figured as much. We don't have a lot of time tonight. Have a seat, and my boy will help you get washed up in a minute. After that, he'll see you get a good meal before you hit the sack."

"Thank you, sir," Callum said, eager to eat yet struggling with hostile feelings toward his new master. The planter's hospitality did nothing to erase the fact that he had knowingly purchased someone else's stolen child.

As if Master Josiah could read his thoughts, he asked, "How loyal are you, Callum? You won't attempt to escape on me, will you now?"

That was an easy question. What prisoner in his right mind would willingly stay on as somebody's slave? Callum didn't appreciate anything that had happened to him. And there was no way he would be Master Josiah's forever slave. The lad had more common sense than to say so. "No, sir. I'll wait right here."

"That you had better," Master Josiah said. "See you in the morning."

Callum watched Master Josiah walk back to his plantation house before venturing inside and sitting on the bed. The shack was dusty, likely due to it having a dirt floor. Cobwebs lined the corners, and a half-decomposed mouse sprawled itself out next to the door.

Callum laid back on the bed for a few seconds before rising to a seated position. At least he had the freedom to move on his own. That was the first time the lad had been able to sit up of his own accord for two months. He repeated the motion several times. That part of being enslaved he could appreciate.

A young man, around seventeen or eighteen, peeked his head through the doorway. "My sniffer tells me my father was right. You're long overdue for a sound scrubbin'. Follow me so you can get washed up."

Hesitantly Callum said, "I... umm... I bathed on the ship this morning."

Unfortunately, that was not the response Master Josiah's son was expecting. He barged into the shack. "I didn't ask any questions, red-leg. You stink!"

Not wanting trouble, Callum put his feet on the floor.

"You'll refer to me as Master Cyrus," the young man said. "Or as just plain Master if you'd rather. Now that we have that settled, let's go!"

Callum was already uncomfortable calling Josiah his master — the idea of referring to Cyrus, someone only a few years older than he, by that title was humiliating. But it was too soon to defy commands, especially ones coming from the planter's son.

Arriving at a creek, Master Cyrus instructed Callum to get out of his nightgown. "My father told me to help you bathe. *Not happening.* You're plenty old enough to handle that on your own. I'm not touching a sorry no good for nothin' red-leg any more than I have to. Hurry up, get those clothes off!"

Callum hated getting naked in front of anybody. He'd have to swallow his pride. Turning his back to Master Cyrus, the lad quickly pulled off his nightgown.

"Finally!" Master Cyrus growled. "Now hop in there and wash off that stench. Don't forget your hair, armpits, or well, just don't forget anywhere. Here's some soap. Use it. *Plenty of it!*"

If there was one thing Callum and Master Cyrus saw eye to eye on, it was that Callum didn't need help bathing. Quite frankly, he was thankful Master Cyrus wanted nothing to do with helping him wash.

Callum dipped his left foot into the water. It was chilly, but he had been in worse. He stepped the rest of the way in and found the water deep enough to reach his shins. Keeping his back to Master Cyrus, the lad knelt down, leaned over, and put his head underwater. Talk about cold!

If getting his head wet accomplished nothing else, it sped up the bathing process. Callum washed his entire body in less than three minutes.

Eager to cover himself back up, he asked for his gown.

"I have clean clothes for you," Master Cyrus said, "But I'm not giving them to you while you're in the water. Come back over here."

Slowly, Callum turned and stepped onto the bank.

Master Cyrus dropped a pair of tan-colored breeches onto the grass between them.

Callum shot him an evil eye while reaching down to pick them up.

"Why, thank you, red-leg! You just gave me the excuse I needed to take the whip to you. You're going to learn real quick on this plantation that red-legs never disrespect their masters. We won't tolerate backtalkin', disobedience, or dirty looks. Let's get you on over to the whippin' post!"

Smartly slipping his breeches on, Callum pleaded with the young man, "Please don't whip me, Master Cyrus. It won't happen again. I promise!"

Master Cyrus grinned, "Nobody's ever whipped you before, have they, red-leg?"

The conversation made Callum as comfortable as a snowman come spring. Tears poured down his cheeks. "No, sir. And I didn't mean to disrespect you, sir. Please give me another chance. I'm begging you."

Master Cyrus peered at the sunset for a moment before returning his eyes to the terrified twelve-year-old. "Consider yourself lucky it's so late. Otherwise, I'd bloody you up good about now. I've got to get in bed, and so do you. So I'm letting you go this time. Give me a cross look like that ever again, and I'll whip you until you're standin' in a pool of blood."

"I won't, Master Cyrus," Callum said with a sniffle. "You have my word."

"I'll count on that, red-leg. Here's a shirt. Put it on, and get back to your cabin. I'll bring your food out as soon as my mother has it ready."

Callum picked up the dingy white shirt. Before putting it on, however, he looked for the nightgown Darcy had made for him. Not seeing it, he mustered up the courage to ask Master Cyrus about it. "Have you seen my clothes, sir?"

Master Cyrus smirked, "You mean that disgusting rag you were wearing? I tossed it in the creek while you had your head underwater. That thing's long gone by now."

It took a lot to make Callum angry, but his temperature rose quickly. That nightgown was the only item of sentimental value he had to his name. Master Cyrus had no right taking it from him.

"I'll catch up to it," he said, starting to run downstream.

"Stop!" Master Cyrus ordered. "You're not going anywhere. I told you that tattered old rag is long gone, and that's where it's going to stay."

Callum wanted to strangle the planter's son with his bare hands and send his dead body downstream or to at least smack that smug look off his face. For a moment, Callum felt like he could cry again. But that look! There was no way he would give Master Cyrus the satisfaction of controlling his emotions. Taking a deep breath and putting his shirt on, he said, "I understand, sir. I'll return to my cabin."

With that, the young men parted company. Callum could tolerate Master Josiah, but Master Cyrus was something else. That lad acted as though he were a royal prince. Like his family was the greatest thing that had ever happened to the colonies. How could anyone be proud that his family was responsible for the theft and torture of innocent children and teenagers?

Callum knew it was wrong to hate, but Master Cyrus was the kind of kid any mother with a brain on her shoulders would have left on somebody's doorstep.

Callum's stomach rumbled all the way back to his cabin, taking his mind off of his master's arrogant son. At least the thought of having supper at his place, as opposed to having food thrown at his face while chained to a shelf, was appealing. Callum didn't care what they fixed him. Anything would do. Sitting on the bed, the only piece of furniture in the cabin, he waited for what seemed like an eternity.

Thirty minutes later, Master Cyrus returned with a plate of chicken, green beans, and mashed potatoes.

Callum's mouth watered, just smelling it. "Thank you, Master Cy—"

Before the lad could finish his sentence, Master Cyrus intentionally dropped his plate on the ground, causing most of the food to fall off into the dirt, "Enjoy!"

How heartlessly cruel! Why would anyone even think of doing something so low? Callum struggled to keep his cool. But he had to. "Oh, I wish you hadn't dropped that," he said. "I was going to see if you wanted to eat with me. Here, I'll see if I can dust the chicken off for you."

As Callum knelt to grab the chicken, Master Cyrus kicked dirt in his face. "Guess it's true what they say about your kind. You really are nothin' but poor-white earth scratching scum."

Fighting even harder to maintain his composure, Callum wiped the dirt from his eyes and mouth, picked up the chicken, and wiped it off on his breeches.

"Don't tear those up," Master Cyrus warned. "They'll have to do you for the next six months. Same for that shirt I brought you."

"Yes, Master Cyrus," Callum said, pretending to hold the low-life in high regard. "I'm sorry, sir," he added while returning to his place on the bed, chicken in hand.

"On the ground, red-leg! There's still food that needs cleanin' up!"

To prevent upsetting the planter's son any further, Callum laid the chicken on the bed and returned to the dirt floor, where he began scooping the potatoes and green beans back onto the plate.

"Eat 'em on your hands and knees like the dog that—"

Master Josiah suddenly appeared out of nowhere. "I was wondering what was taking you so long, Cyrus! Callum, sit on your bed and eat that chicken before it cools off any more than it already has. Cyrus, pick up every bean, clean it off, and put it back on his plate. Those potatoes aren't going to come clean, so tomorrow morning, I'm giving your portion of breakfast to Callum."

If Master Cyrus were anything like Sullivan, he'd find a way to smooth talk himself out of this one. He'd claim Callum had spilled his own food. To the lad's surprise, Master Cyrus began cleaning off the beans without uttering as much as a peep as his father continued. "I'll skin you alive if I catch you mistreating Callum or any of our other servants for that matter. Do I make myself clear?"

"Yes, sir," Master Cyrus said.

Master Josiah didn't leave the cabin until every last bean had been cleaned off and handed back to Callum. "Apologize to him," he ordered.

Master Cyrus blushed.

"Now, Cyrus!"

"Sorry for havin' a little fun with you, red-leg."

Master Josiah smacked him on the back of the head, "A real apology! Now, son!"

Master Cyrus cracked his knuckles for a few seconds before making eye contact with

Callum, "I apologize for treatin' you the way I did. There's no excuse for my behavior."

"I'll agree with you on that one," Master Josiah said.

CHAPTER SIX

THE SWEET SOUND OF VENGEANCE

A gentle head rub woke Callum from his sleep. Next to his bed stood a lady whose smile lines reminded him of Darcy's. "Good morning," she whispered.

Callum stretched both arms over his head, "Good morning to you, ma'am."

"I'm Mistress Rosanna, Josiah's—"

Bursting through the door behind her, Master Cyrus shouted, "Don't you be sleepin' all day, red-leg! There's much work to do! Get out of—"

Mistress Rosanna pressed a finger against her lips while awarding Master Cyrus an evil glare.

"I was just—"

"Cyrus, baby, bite that vile tongue of yours before I speak with your father about your sassiness!"

"Sorry, ma'am."

That was not the reaction Callum had anticipated. But he liked it!

Mistress Rosanna patted Callum's knee a couple of times, "Excuse my ill-mannered son. He spoke the truth, but his rude manners were entirely unacceptable. Mornings come early on a tobacco plantation. From now on, you'll be expected at the plantation house just before sun-up each morning for breakfast. As soon as the light breaks, you'll join our other servants in hoeing the fields or whatever other duties you're assigned. Since it's your first morning, I kept your breakfast warm. Come over to the house, and you can eat."

Master Cyrus had managed to keep quiet for a minute. But it didn't last long. "You're going to let that red-leg get away with—"

Mistress Rosanna snapped her fingers and pointed toward the door. Master Cyrus stopped speaking mid-sentence. "Welcome to the Gillcrest plantation, Callum," Mistress Rosanna continued. "Excuse Cyrus and I as we return to the house for a word with his father. If you want to eat, come along promptly."

Callum liked Mistress Rosanna. She was kind. Not only that, but she didn't take anything off of her bratty son.

Scooting out of bed, the lad wondered how deep of trouble Master Cyrus would be in. He hoped Master Josiah would thrash the seat right out of his son's trousers. That boy needed to be brought down a peg or two.

Callum was in a hurry to eat yet was somewhat apprehensive of dining in the main plantation house, having no idea how many other slaves were there or how he would be treated. Callum had never liked crowds, but that wasn't his only problem. Master Cyrus was undoubtedly going to make his life miserable. He wanted to stay as far away from the planter's son as he possibly could.

After nervously pacing back and forth through his cabin for a couple of minutes, the lad forced himself to leave the confines of his slave shack. The dew-covered grass was cold on bare feet, but it wasn't anything Callum couldn't adjust to. And that aroma rolling out of the plantation house — Mmm... Mmm.

Master Cyrus met Callum at the door with a smile, and not a mischievous one. In an unexpected move, he said, "Thank you for comin' over so quickly. Follow me inside, and I'll seat you in the dining room."

Callum hadn't delayed long enough for Master Cyrus to have gotten a whipping. Still, he suspected the older teenager knew he had one coming and was likely on his best behavior in hopes of lightening the punishment.

The dining room was unlike any Callum had ever seen. It was three times the size of the living room he and his siblings slept in back in Dublin. That thought got his brain working overtime. Where had the people-thieves taken his siblings? Would he ever see them again? For that matter, had the rogues sent his parents somewhere, or had they killed them? But worrying about things he had no control over was useless. That's what Darcy always told him anyway.

Master Cyrus pulled a chair out from the table and motioned for Callum to sit in it.

The twelve-year-old nervously complied.

"Make yourself comfortable," the planter's son said. "I'll return with your breakfast in a second."

What a remarkable transformation of character! Something had happened. Callum just wondered what it had been. Quietly, he tip-toed to the doorway.

"You're doing just fine," Mistress Rosanna was telling Master Cyrus. "Keep it up, baby."

"Is Father serious about making me work in the field with that red-leg *all day*?"

"Your father would never jest about such a matter, baby, and you know it. Now march Callum's food in there before it cools."

Hearing that, Callum rushed back to his seat and pretended he had been sitting there the entire time.

An enormous johnnycake, a couple of sausage patties, a handful of fried potatoes, and some ice-cold water to wash it down! Not only that but he was being waited on hand and foot! Never had he been treated so well in Dublin.

Reaching for one of those mouth-watering johnnycakes, Callum was startled when Master Cyrus firmly grabbed hold of his wrist. "Don't eat before asking God's blessin' on your food!"

Callum stared at him blankly. Sure, he'd heard of God. And he'd heard some folks believed He was real. He had even heard of saying prayers before eating and at bedtime and all. But Master Cyrus? A man of prayer? That was about as likely as a blacksmith trying to build an igloo in the middle of the desert!

"There's nothin' to it," Master Cyrus went on. "Put your head down like this."

After a moment of hesitation, Callum complied.

Master Cyrus released an annoyed sigh, "Close your eyes and say, 'Dear God, thank you for the food You've set before me.' After that, ask Him to bless it and help it nourish your body. Then say 'Amen,' and you can eat."

Prayer, the way Callum understood it, was sort of like poetry. He just had to memorize some words and then quote them with his nose pointed toward the floor and his eyes shut. It didn't make much sense, but he could manage if that were the proper way.

After quoting the prayer-poem, Callum said, "There, how was that?"

Master Cyrus nodded, "Fine. Hurry up and eat."

Smiling, Callum grabbed that johnnycake with both hands and took a giant bite out of it. It was divine! As he continued chowing down, his mind began to wander. If it were customary for the Gillcrests to say prayer-poems before they ate, why hadn't anybody told him that before he ate the chicken the night before? Perhaps some questions were better off unasked.

Immediately after taking the last crumb off his plate, Master Cyrus snatched Callum's dish. "Don't go anywhere. More's on the way."

More? Callum hadn't eaten that much food in months! Already stuffed to the gills, he didn't know how he'd find room for anything else. But he wasn't about to shy away from the challenge either.

While Master Cyrus was in the kitchen, Callum perused the dining room. Up until that moment, he assumed Master Cyrus was an only child. But those pictures on the walls told a different story altogether. It didn't make sense, though. If there were more kids in the family, where were they all? And why was the house so quiet?

Master Cyrus slid another dish beneath Callum's nose. A plate piled even higher than the first had been.

"Don't expect two helpings for every meal. This is the portion I was supposed to eat. But Father said I have to watch you enjoy it because of what happened last night."

That's right! How had Callum forgotten? Darcy used to tell him vengeance had a sweet sound to it. Licking his lips, he said, "Thank you, Master Cyrus. This is the best breakfast I've ever had!"

Determined to make Master Cyrus regret the foolish decision he'd made the night before, Callum brought a sausage patty to his nose and gave it a good whiff, "Sausage has always been one of my favorites."

Master Cyrus did not appreciate his antics. "Hurry up," he grumbled. "You've got work to do."

Mistress Rosanna corrected him from the kitchen, "Don't you mean, *'We've* got work to do?"

"Oh yeah," Master Cyrus said. "Father wants me to work the field with you today. You know, to show you the ropes since you don't know what you're doin.'"

Callum grinned, inwardly reminding himself that the best way to annoy a guy like Master Cyrus was with a kindness shower. "I'll be looking forward to it. Hopefully, we'll get to work together every day."

Master Cyrus whispered, "Don't forget who's in charge here, red-leg. Hurry up and finish that breakfast *before I cram it down your throat!*"

Well, that settled that! Right when Callum was starting to think good ole Master Cyrus was coming down with influenza or something, he snapped back to his old self again. Callum nodded in silence and rushed through the rest of his meal.

"Wait right here. Now I have to wash your dishes. When I finish, I'll come out and get you so we can get out to the field."

"Yes, sir," Callum said, pushing his plate forward, hoping it would take Master Cyrus a while to get those dishes done. If he didn't get some of that food digested, there was no way he would be able to work. His stomach hurt so badly that he wasn't even sure if he'd be able to stand.

The front door opened, and in tromped Master Josiah. "Morning there, Callum. Cyrus in the kitchen?"

"Yes, sir. And good morning."

Master Josiah took his broad-brimmed hat off and hustled into the other room, "What's the hold-up, son? You've got three minutes to get those dishes washed, dried, and put away! Three minutes. Do you hear me?"

"Yes, sir," Master Cyrus said.

That Master Cyrus sure was a difficult one to figure out. He was as mean as a snake when it came to how he treated Callum. But his parents, especially his father, could order him to do something, and he'd comply as if he were the perfect gentleman.

"Callum!" Master Josiah called. "Join us in the kitchen, please."

So good to sitting still and allowing his food to digest! Trying to stay on Master Josiah's good side, Callum jumped up, shoved his chair under the table, and hurried to the kitchen.

"Callum, I'm about to give my son instructions for the day. It's only fitting for you to be here for this conversation."

Master Cyrus busied himself drying dishes yet making eye contact with his father the entire time the man spoke. "Cyrus, you're in for a rough day. Your mother and I talked last night, and the best way we can think of to teach you to appreciate our servants is to not only have you work the field alongside Callum but to have you *become* a servant for a day."

Master Cyrus set down the tankard he was working on and appeared to stop breathing for a second.

"Today, you and Callum will be equals. Callum, for the rest of the day, you can drop the title of 'master' when referring to Cyrus. And

Cyrus, for the rest of the day, refer to Callum by name only."

Master Cyrus picked the tankard back up and finished drying it.

"I'm going to assign both of you to weed the north field. I don't want to find either one of you slacking. You'll work until I announce it's time for lunch. And of course, after lunch, you'll work some more."

Mistress Rosanna interrupted, "Cyrus, baby, I'll finish up the dishes. You guys better get out there and start weeding."

"Yes, ma'am. Thank you," Master Cyrus said. "Come on then, *Callum.* I'll show you the way."

CHAPTER SEVEN

THE DEAL

Never in his life had Callum worked so vigorously. That hoe handle was vicious, leaving him with splinters and blisters on both hands. His back ached. And the sun was anything but considerate of his fair skin. From his calves down to his ankles, the lad was burned to a crisp. At least now he understood why everybody called him a red-leg.

Just ahead, Master Cyrus was working away. Somehow Callum felt Master Cyrus was every bit as out-of-shape and sore as he was. Being the planter's son, it was doubtful he was used to performing such strenuous labor. If that were the case, though, he certainly knew how to put on a show. The boy hadn't taken a break in hours.

Raking his hoe across the ground again, Callum wished he could suppress the thoughts constantly coming to mind. Thoughts like whether or not his siblings and parents were still among the living. Thoughts like whether or not he should run off to explore neighboring plantations in case someone in the community had purchased any of his relatives. Thoughts about why Uncle Keir hadn't come to his rescue.

In the distance, Callum heard and occasionally caught sight of other servants tending tobacco crops. There were half a dozen or so of them — far less than the number Callum would have expected.

If only the sun had hidden behind a cloud for even five minutes, Callum would have been most grateful. Sweat streamed down his face. Never before had he felt so dehydrated. Still, he worked. It was, after all, only his first day of being there, and the fear of what might happen if he failed to do his job was enough to keep him moving.

Callum's belly growled. Surely it was past lunchtime. For a second, he placed his hand on his stomach. A second was all it took. Unbeknownst to him, a yellowjacket had been resting half an inch above his belly button. As soon as his hand made contact, it stung him. "Ayy!" he hissed.

Master Cyrus turned around. "Stop makin' such a fuss and start workin'!"

"A bee got me!" Callum hollered back, dropping the hoe and rubbing the welt on his tummy.

Master Cyrus shot him an evil eye, "He was tellin' you you're not workin' fast enough. Better get back to it before another one gets you."

Even the bees helped enforce job assignments? That was a chilling thought. Callum knew Master Cyrus might have simply been making fun of him, but everything in the colonies was so different than things were back in Dublin that he didn't know what to believe.

Forcing himself to overlook the pain, Callum picked the hoe back up and continued chopping weeds for another hour before Master Josiah appeared. "You've got twenty-five minutes to get back to the plantation house, eat, and return to your position. Not a minute more!"

As far from the house as they were, the only way to get there and back that fast was to run as if they were being chased by a flock of demon-possessed geese, grab the food, and gobble it down while running back to their work area. The plan was less than ideal, but following Master Cyrus's lead, Callum bolted toward the plantation house with his bare feet finding every rock and twig along the way.

As they ran, Master Cyrus held the lead. Having a competitive spirit, Callum was determined to show him who was boss. He might not have been able to catch up on the way to the house, but he would make up the time in getting his food and returning to work. That he was certain of!

Grabbing a small trout and an ear of corn with his left hand and a tankard of water with his right, the lad wasted no time in heading back to the field. Within seconds of beginning his run, he heard fast-moving footsteps coming behind him. Without even looking, he knew they belonged to Master Cyrus. That boy must have shared his desire for dominance. He was gaining ground quicker than Callum thought possible.

Ignoring the pain in his feet and the soreness of his muscles, Callum sprinted, forgetting about his lunch. But Master Cyrus had an unfair advantage — shoes. Still, for three-quarters of the way, Callum kept him at bay. And he would have kept it that way had he not tripped over his own two feet, sending his food and water airborne.

"Poor-white red-leg," Master Cyrus scoffed, barreling past him.

During the fall, Callum scraped his hands and knees, losing the small amount of water that hadn't already splashed out while running. He punched the ground with a closed fist before picking up the trout and corn and hurriedly limping back toward his spot in the field.

By the time he arrived, Master Cyrus was already pulling weeds. Glancing around to make sure no one was within earshot, Callum pressed him, "Cyrus, what will your father think when he finds out you called me a poor-white red-leg? You know he said you couldn't call me by anything other than my name today."

Master Cyrus dropped his hoe and charged at Callum like a raging bull. In a move unanticipated by the lad, the planter's son punched him in the throat, temporarily making him feel like he was going to die. While Callum struggled to breathe, Master Cyrus shoved him to the ground, jumped on top of him, and pounded his face, leaving him with a bloody nose and swollen lips. "Tattle on that!"

Callum's hatred for Master Cyrus was rapidly intensifying. Yes, he should have kept his mouth shut. But they were words. It wasn't like he had stolen the guy's girlfriend. According to Darcy, words never excused violence.

Ever-so-slowly, Callum returned to his feet and brushed himself off. Glancing at his hoe, he thought of something he would rather do with it than pull weeds. But he knew better. The planter's son had already returned to work but was likely watching him through the corner of his eye. He would have to launch an attack when the monster least expected it.

Callum picked up his future weapon and resumed using it as a garden tool. One thing was for sure — he wouldn't have to snitch on Master Cyrus now. Master Josiah or Mistress Rosanna would undoubtedly notice the marks on his face, and when they did, somebody was going to be on the receiving end of severe discipline. Hopefully, the consequences wouldn't involve the two working together for another day or longer. The less he had to see of the planter's son, the better.

For three hours, neither of the young men spoke. But silence can only last so long. "Rain's movin' in," Master Cyrus said.

Callum thought his first words would have been something like, "I'm sorry for attacking you," or at least, "Are you okay?" Ignoring his statement, Callum continued working quietly.

"Did you hear me?" Master Cyrus asked. "*I said*, rain's movin' in."

Callum hoed another clump of weeds.

Master Cyrus walked back to him, "I'll let you in on a little secret. My father bought you *for me*."

Not liking the sound of that, Callum stopped hoeing and glanced up at him.

"Yeah, I knew you could hear me. Right now, I'm under my father's authority. He's allowin' me to be in charge of you to a certain degree. But he's greatly limitin' how far I can take things. When you're mine, and those restrictions are lifted, I won't hesitate to tear *every* inch of flesh off you, red-leg. If you have an ounce of intelligence, you'll do everything in your power to make me happy. Now, let's try this again... Rain's movin' in."

Trembling, Callum replied, "I see that, Master Cyrus."

The planter's son patted him on the head as if he were a dog, "Better. When anybody asks what happened to your face, tell 'em you got tired of workin' in the sun and attempted to run away. I chased after you; you shoved me down and took off runnin'. I got up and came after you a second time, and you started throwin' rocks at me. I gave you a sound beatin' to keep you from runnin' off and to teach you not to rebel against your authority figures, and that's all there was to it."

Callum may have been new to plantation life and being a slave, but he was smart enough to recognize the dangers associated with telling such a story as Master Cyrus had crafted. "What's the punishment for running away?"

"Depends on the slave," Master Cyrus said.

"What do you mean?"

"For a first offense, a smoked Irish would have the shirt ripped off his back and be given a harsh whipping in front of the other slaves. But for poor-whites, it depends. In the worst-case scenario, a red-leg could be burned alive."

Callum swallowed hard, "What's a smoked Irish?"

"Enough with the questions. Tell my father about me callin' you a poor-white red-leg or about me beatin' you up for threatening to tell on me, and when you're officially my slave, I'll give you the whippin' of a lifetime on day one. And probably on days two, three, four, and five as well. Go along with the story I told you, and

I'll do my best to keep him from taking the whip to you."

"Let me make sure I understand this," Callum said. "If I tell the truth, your father is going to—"

"You lads are supposed to be working!" Master Josiah thundered, storming toward the young men. "Stop those mouths, and get the weeds out of there!"

"Yes, sir!" Master Cyrus called before whispering, "Just do what I told you."

"Yes, sir! Sorry, sir!" Callum called out, still unsure what he might say when confronted by Master Josiah. If he told the truth and Master Josiah believed him, Master Cyrus would suffer his father's wrath. But what if Master Josiah didn't believe him? What would be worse? Saying he tried to run away and Master Cyrus stopped him? Or telling the truth and being thought a liar? Either way was likely to fetch dire consequences.

Master Josiah continued his path toward the boys. "Not bad," he said. "You've missed a few, so one of you needs to come back here and — Callum, what happened to you?"

Callum shrunk back in fear. Anything he said would likely result in physical torment he wasn't ready for, either at the hands of Master

Cyrus or at the hands of Master Josiah, or possibly both.

"He tried to run away," Master Cyrus answered for him.

Master Josiah's face hardened. "And why, Callum, would you do such a thing?"

Taking a deep breath, Callum knew there was no getting out of this. He needed a clever response. Closing his eyes for a few seconds, he said, "Look at my hands; the blisters keep breaking open. Not only that, but I've got a bad sunburn, and I'm hurting all over."

Master Josiah looked disappointed, "You took off because it was too much work?"

Callum looked toward the ground.

"Bring your eyes up here to meet mine. Is that why you tried to run?"

Callum nodded and said a quiet, "Yes, sir."

"Do you know how serious punishments can be for runaway slaves?"

"Ye.. yes, sir," Callum stammered.

Josiah gripped the lad's shoulder, "Come with me then!"

Terror-stricken, Callum turned his eyes toward the planter's son, hoping he would jump to his defense.

At first, Master Cyrus watched silently as his father marched Callum toward the plantation house. Callum's internal temperature was on the rise. If he hadn't already made a false confession, he would have squealed. But doing so now would only make him get twice the punishment. That he was sure of.

"Father," Master Cyrus suddenly blurted out, "May I have a word with you?"

"Make it quick," Master Josiah snapped. "It's time for this lad to learn his place."

"Father, please don't be upset with me for sayin' this, but I believe Callum's already learned his lesson. He's gonna feel that black eye and those swollen lips for a week or two. He's not goin' anywhere."

Master Josiah raised one eyebrow. "Since when do you care what happens to a red-leg?"

Callum could feel his chest tightening. Master Cyrus might not be able to get him out of this. A tear trickled down his cheek as he pictured himself being lit on fire and burned alive.

"He's younger than most of the ones we've had," Master Cyrus said. "And I was slightly rougher on him than I intended to be."

"Are you sure he's not going to take off again?"

"Yes, sir," Master Cyrus replied without hesitation.

"I'll forgive the trespass under one condition, and this is it. If I don't punish the lad now and he attempts to run away in the future, I'll hitch both of you to the whipping post, and each of you will receive thirty lashes."

Master Cyrus's eyes moved upwards and to the left. Callum knew the look. Master Cyrus was struggling to know what to do.

"Do we have an agreement?" Master Josiah asked.

"I don't know, father. Getting thirty lashes because of somethin' a red-leg does?"

"It's up to you, Cyrus. Either he gets twelve lashes now, and you have nothing to worry about, or one of two things will happen. You've either taught him a lesson, and he won't run, meaning nobody gets a whipping. Or he runs again, and you both get a strong dose of the whip. What's it going to be?"

Master Cyrus attempted to negotiate, "What about this? Instead of thirty lashes, what if I agree to a different form of punishment? Like to work as a slave for a week?"

"A lashing for both," Master Josiah insisted. "This is not something I'm willing to compromise on."

Callum didn't like the direction of this conversation. If roles were reversed, he knew what he would say. That's what scared him.

After a few more seconds of silence, Master Cyrus made one final attempt, "Could mine be done in private with your belt or a switch instead of the whip?"

"You're not in a position to bargain here, Cyrus. I already told you that. Are you going to accept the offer or reject it?"

"I don't know," Master Cyrus said. "Those are tough terms. I have no way of knowin' what this red-leg might do in the future."

"Very well then," Master Josiah said. "Let's go, Callum! Twelve lashes it is."

Tears welled up in Callum's eyes. He hadn't done anything wrong, yet he was about to get beaten to a bloody pulp. It was Master Cyrus who deserved to have his skin torn, not him. Seeing the whipping post off in the distance, Callum's tears began flowing. He would have run had Master Josiah not had such a firm grip on his shoulder.

"I'll accept the offer!" Master Cyrus called out after them.

What? Surely Callum hadn't heard that right. Master Cyrus was anything but a sympathetic, compassionate kind of person. Sometimes Callum even doubted he was human. Why would he, of all people, put himself in harm's way for someone he clearly detested?

"Thirty lashes in front of everyone with a whip?" Master Josiah continued.

"Yes, sir," Master Cyrus agreed. Sounding confident, he added, "I'll see to it that he doesn't run again."

CHAPTER EIGHT

INTERNAL ENEMY

The pitter-patter of a rodent scurrying back and forth across the dirt floor of Callum's shack put the lad on edge. When he lived in Dublin, a mouse woke his sister up one night, attempting to wrench hairs right out of her head. Callum hoped mice in the colonies would be slightly more mannerly than the ones back at home.

Sitting up on his bed, Callum hugged his knees to his chest. Pitter-patter, pitter-patter, pitter-patter. The longer he listened, the less it sounded like a mouse and the more like a rat. A rabid one with a long, curly tail, oversized buck teeth, a fat tummy, and beady eyes.

Fear was an enemy worth defeating. That's what Darcy had always told him. Callum had to stop envisioning the critter as a ferocious rat longing to draw blood. Squeezing his eyelids shut, he forced himself to see her with a smile on her face, crinkling her adorable pink little nose as she peered around the room, searching for fallen crumbs or at least a warm place to sleep. He couldn't fault the poor girl for trying to survive, could he?

It wasn't like that little rodent was a real rat anyway. The real rat was none other than Master Cyrus Gillcrest. The thought of being owned by a young, arrogant, cruel-hearted heathen was nearly more than he could bear. Master Cyrus didn't deserve to own any slaves. If he deserved anything, it was to become worm food deposited in an early grave.

Callum remembered that hoe he had been holding earlier in the day. He had refrained himself because Master Cyrus was at least halfway behaving like a slave himself. But tomorrow, when that sun came over the mountain, things would be different. Master Cyrus would be back on his high horse, and Callum would undoubtedly become the object of his power-loving brutality. Callum brought his fingers up to his swollen lip, then rubbed the bruise on his cheek.

The planter's son was an interesting character. Callum wondered why he behaved the way he did. What was he so angry about? Why did he enjoy intimidating people who were smaller than him? For that matter, why should Callum believe he was telling the truth about one day becoming the lad's true master? He was probably making the whole thing up!

What if he was telling the truth? Having every inch of his flesh torn off was not a threat that could be easily ignored. But what would Callum's parents think about having a murderer for a son? What about his siblings? Or Darcy? What would they think? Would it make a difference if he killed Master Cyrus in self-defense?

Maybe the lad could try that whole prayer-poem thing again. Bowing his head and closing his eyes, Callum said, "Dear God, thank you for this food you've set before me."

Suddenly, the lad understood the prayer-poem he had recited only made sense when spoken before a meal. He would have to ask Master Cyrus which prayer-poem would be appropriate for — on second thought, maybe that wasn't such a bright idea.

Perhaps the best thing the twelve-year-old could do was get a decent night's rest. The morning would be there before he knew what hit him, and he would need all the energy he could muster. Callum closed his eyes again. Pitter-patter. Pitter-patter. Pitter-patter. He couldn't believe he'd so easily forgotten about the rodent. She had been quiet all of that time. The only reason she was scurrying around again was because she knew he was trying to get some sleep. Stupid critter!

Callum smacked the wall and hollered, "Go away, you varmint! I don't want you here!"

Those were the wrong words to say. Callum had heard them before. Too many times to count. "I don't want you here" may not have been the exact same words he had heard, but they were close enough. In Dublin, low-income Irish families were appreciated as much as dog manure on the bottom of one's shoe. Callum couldn't count the number of poor folks who had been arrested for littering or being late paying a debt and then disappeared without explanation. At least, if there had been an explanation, the adult McCarthys had kept it from their children.

A lump formed in Callum's throat. Sometimes he wished he had never been born. Perhaps his life was nothing more than a mistake that should have never happened. Darcy always said everyone who was born had a purpose. Perhaps Callum's only purpose was to absorb the anger and ridicule of others. Somehow, that wasn't comforting. Maybe it was Callum who needed that early grave.

A tear trickled down the lad's cheek. Life seemed so overwhelming at times. Why couldn't he and Master Cyrus switch places? That would be the day!

Callum ran his fingers through his hair, mumbling, "I've got to stop thinking this way. It's not good for me."

More tears streamed down his face. Tears of hopelessness, confusion, and anger. Callum's emotions were overtaking him, and there was nothing he could do about it.

Rolling onto his stomach, the lad scrunched his fingers into angry cannonballs and repeatedly punched his bed. "I hate my life. It's not fair! No one should have to live this way! I hate it! I hate it! I hate it!"

A sudden gust of cold wind shut him up. Callum lifted his head to find his door wide open. Terrified of getting his first whipping for making such a fuss, he whispered, "Sorry for disturbing you, Master Cyrus."

There was no answer.

"Master Josiah?"

Still, no response.

"Who's there?"

Callum's pulse raced as he ever-so-slowly stood to his feet and tip-toed to the door. "Is anybody out there?"

CHAPTER NINE

HARD CHOICES

Callum nearly leaped out of his skin! His eyes popped open faster than they had the night when he was kidnapped off his living room floor. Drenched from nose to belly button and freezing, he found Master Cyrus towering over him with a mischievous grin on his face and an empty pail in hand. "I warned you before; you can't be sleepin' all day! You've done missed breakfast! Get on your feet and out to that field!"

Through chattering teeth, Callum said, "ye... ye... yes, sir. Sa... sa... sorry, sir."

"Don't waste any more of my time!" Master Cyrus grabbed Callum's arm and jerked him off the bed. "Get dressed in thirty seconds or less, or you're gonna work just like you are!"

Without a word, Callum pulled his clothes on.

"If you haven't figured it out, you poor-white earth scratching scum, we're not equals anymore."

Callum didn't need a reminder. He had worried about it all night. He didn't even know he had fallen asleep until that cold water poured all over him.

All the way to his assigned part of the field, Callum was on the receiving end of a lecture he thought would never end. "Yesterday, you got off easy. You got your little face messed up because you mouthed off to somebody twice your size. You're not in your miserable part of the world anymore, red-leg. People in the colonies won't put up with your nonsense. You're lucky a whip didn't tear the hide off of you. I know you're just a lad, but I promise you this much. You are my opportunity to prove to my father that I'm a man. That I have what it takes to handle my own plantation. That I can keep a red-leg like you workin' those fields. I'm in the mood to prove myself by takin' a whip to somebody. Not to just *anybody*. But to a twelve-year-old lad from Dublin. Today might be your day, red-leg. I'm gonna watch you like a hawk. The first time I catch you wastin' time, lookin' at anybody the wrong way, or even belching or farting, I'm gonna use that as an excuse to whip the daylights out of you!"

The lecture, warnings, and threats continued throughout the long walk to the field. Eventually, Callum tuned Master Cyrus out and delved into thought about the previous night's activities; the ideas of murder and suicide, the mouse scurrying around the room, the door flinging open with no signs of anyone around.

"Do you understand me, red-leg?" Master Cyrus asked, snapping the lad back into the present.

Hoping he hadn't missed anything important, Callum nodded, "Yes, sir."

"Good." Master Cyrus pulled something shiny out of his pocket. "Go ahead and get started, and don't take any breaks until my father or I come along and tell you it's time for lunch. And what are you staring at?"

Callum wasn't sure if he should give an honest answer or not. Shifting his gaze, he looked Master Cyrus in the eye.

"You act like you've never seen a pocket watch before."

The condescending tone of Master Cyrus's voice got under Callum's skin. It wasn't his fault no one in his family had one of those gadgets. He wanted to take a closer look at that thing, and he would find a way to do that later on. For the moment, though, he said, "Of course I've seen a pocket watch. There was a bug on your shirt, and it distracted me for a second. Sorry about that."

Master Cyrus didn't acknowledge his comment. Tucking his watch back into his trouser pocket, he said, "Don't forget what I said. I'll be checkin' on you frequently today." He grinned, "I sure would appreciate it if you'd do somethin' worthy of a good whippin.'"

Handling that statement would be tricky. Saying "Yes, sir" would imply he would intentionally do something to earn himself a whipping. Not saying anything at all might be considered disrespectful, and he would get thrashed anyway. Choosing his words carefully, Callum said, "I won't take any breaks, Master Cyrus. I'll work as hard as I know how, sir."

Master Cyrus chuckled again, "Too bad *your* hardest might not be good enough for me. Get to it, red-leg!"

Callum faked a smile and began hoeing the tobacco field. He wondered how much money the Gillcrests would bring in thanks to his efforts. And how much would go to buy nice things for Master Cyrus.

The planter's son glared intently at the lad for the first few minutes, making Callum doubt he would get through the morning without a beating. If he got one, it wasn't going to be because he did anything wrong but on account of the egotistical hothead who was supervising him.

After a short while, Master Cyrus pulled out the pocket watch again. Looking at it, he said, "I've got some things to take care of, red-leg. I'll be back shortly."

What a shame! Callum had so been looking forward to being gawked at the entire time he worked. *Not!*

Ten minutes after Master Cyrus moved on, the hoe handle busted open a large blister just below Callum's ring finger. It stung, and with the handle constantly bumping up against it, the pain intensified quickly, but the lad knew that pain would pale in comparison to what he would suffer if he didn't get back to work. He hoed, and hoed, and hoed some more. With sweat dripping down his forehead and his filthy shirt clinging to his back, Callum struggled to ignore his exhaustion from a lack of sleep, his unhappy stomach, and his soreness from the previous day's activities. Still yet, staying on his feet was quite the challenge.

The one thing he was thankful for was that Master Cyrus wasn't staying right on top of him as he had threatened to do. He was entirely out of sight — at least for the moment.

With a growling stomach and a throbbing headache, Callum steadily worked the field, hating Master Cyrus and his own new life on the plantation more and more as the day went on. He needed somebody to talk to. Somebody to encourage him. Either that, or he needed to get rid of Master Cyrus once and for all. Maybe he would be better off running away to regain his freedom.

"Stop thinking that way," a gruff voice warned.

Callum turned to see a black slave he guessed to be in his mid-thirties. "Runaway white niggers always get caught; when they do, most of 'em never consider runnin' again."

"Are you talking to me? I'm not a white nigger. And I didn't say anything about running away."

"Oh, but you thought it, lad. And you *are* a white nigger. You just don't know it yet."

"I wasn't thinking of running away."

"You're not a very good liar, boy. You don't have to tell me the truth. But know this — if you get caught, I mean *when* you get caught, the Gillcrests will beat you within an inch of your life, and when they're finished, they'll put chains around your legs and attach a heavy collar to your neck, and you'll have to work that way for years to come. It ain't worth it."

The black slave walked away, leaving Callum to ponder his words. He wondered how that man knew what he had been thinking about. If nothing else, at least he would have a chance to talk to somebody in a similar predicament to his own.

He continued hoeing the field while beating himself up for not at least asking the man his name. Perhaps he would have a chance to talk with him again in the near future.

Callum hoed that field so hard and for so long that he feared he might faint. He was beginning to think Master Cyrus had utterly forgotten about him. That is until the young master stomped over and firmly gripped his shoulder, "You haven't been slackin' off on your work, have you, there, red-leg?"

"No, sir," Callum replied.

"I'm not so sure," Master Cyrus countered. "Doesn't look like you've gotten much accomplished. Did I see you talkin' to one of those Smoked Irish a few minutes ago?"

Smoked Irish? Now Callum got it. That was the term the planters used in reference to the black slaves. "I wasn't talkin' to anybody, and I've been working as hard as—"

Master Cyrus backhanded the lad, busting the corner of his lip again. "I told you this mornin'; I won't tolerate any disrespect. Don't lie to or talk back to me, you poor-white earth scratching scum. You have twenty-five minutes to get your food, eat, and get back here. You better not be as much as a minute late. And when you return, I expect you to work double-time. I'll tolerate nothing less! Now, go!"

Callum didn't know how he would run on an empty stomach with no energy, but he didn't have much choice. Turning, he ran with all his might, guzzled a third of a tankard of water, crammed a piece of cornbread in his mouth, and rushed back to the field, where Master Cyrus was waiting.

"Two minutes late, red-leg."

"Master Cyrus, I went—"

Master Cyrus backhanded him a second time. "What's it gonna take to get you to learn, red-leg? You can't talk back to your master. No matter your excuse, you're two minutes late. That means you defied me." Master Cyrus paused for effect before faking a creepy laugh. "And do you know what that means?"

Master Cyrus had that sinister look in his eye again. It sent a shiver down Callum's spine. "Please don't whip me," the lad begged.

Grinning, Master Cyrus excitedly rubbed his hands together.

"Please, sir," Callum begged, falling to his knees.

"I don't know. If I keep cuttin' you slack, you're gonna become far too unruly. I can't have that."

Callum's entire body began to tremble, and a monsoon of tears poured down his face. "I won't disappoint you again. Please, sir. Please don't. I'm begging you."

Master Cyrus chuckled. "Look me in the eye, red-leg."

Callum quietly complied.

"You've got two choices. Would you rather have the whip taken to you or forfeit your supper by workin' through it tonight?"

CHAPTER TEN
THE DISCOVERY

For the first time since beginning to work at the Gillcrest plantation, Callum was the first to arrive for breakfast. Going to bed on an empty stomach made it much easier to wake up not only on time but early. He was determined to get three good meals that day to help him with his work assignments.

Mistress Rosanna greeted him at the door, "Good morning, Callum. Breakfast isn't quite ready yet. Go ahead and set the table."

"Yes, ma'am. If you don't mind me asking, what's for breakfast? It smells wonderful!"

Mistress Rosanna smiled, "We're having porridge, bannock, and on account of it being

Sunday, we're going to have Indian pudding on the side."

Callum had no idea what any of that was, but he couldn't wait to find out. He wasted no time in setting the table. The way he figured it, the faster that table was set, the quicker he could eat.

Master Cyrus strutted through the kitchen, gazing downward while fastening his suspenders. "I'm headin' out to check on my new charge. If that red-leg's not up and on his way over here, I'm gonna—"

"Cyrus, Callum is right here, baby," Mistress Rosanna interrupted.

"I know you think I'm bein' rough on him, but he has to learn to—"

"Baby," Mistress Rosanna interrupted again. "You didn't listen to a word I said, did you?"

For the first time, Master Cyrus raised his head. "Red-leg? You're up early. I'm assumin' that means you know it's Sunday?"

"Yes, sir," Callum replied. "Mistress Rosanna told me."

Master Cyrus gave him a dirty look. "She did, did she?"

"Calm down, Cyrus," Mistress Rosanna said. "He got himself up and came over here completely on his own. Baby, I'm beginning to worry about you. You almost sound disappointed that Callum's here. Almost like you were hoping to rough him up."

Master Cyrus grinned but didn't speak.

"Callum," Mistress Rosanna added, "I don't know if anybody has shared this with you or not, but Sundays belong to the Lord, and they're days when we allow our servants to rest from all their labors."

Young Callum could barely believe his ears. Every Sunday off? That might give his hands a chance to heal and his tense muscles an opportunity to relax. Six days of work and one day of rest was something he could handle.

Callum glanced at the people-sketches while he waited. An unhappy young girl caught his eye. She was the only girl in any of the pictures who wore a ribbon in her hair. Sitting on a bale of hay, the little one was cradling a baby doll while staring into space.

Callum had been on the Gillcrest plantation for a few days and had still heard no talk of Master Cyrus having siblings. Yet those drawings made it clear he had some. Where were they?

"Why do you keep lookin' around the room like that?" Master Cyrus asked. "Are you tryin' to find somethin' to steal?"

"No, sir. I would never do that. I was just wondering where your brothers and sisters are."

"Brothers and sisters? Who said I have any?"

"There are drawings of them everywhere."

Master Cyrus chuckled, "You're a nosy little red-leg, aren't you? Mother made those drawings of me with my cousins. I don't have any siblings."

Callum may have been only twelve-years-old, but he was far from stupid. Regardless of how confident Master Cyrus pretended to be, his voice cracked. Not only that, but Mistress Rosanna intentionally avoided their conversation. Callum was sure their behavior was anything but coincidental. The Gillcrests were hiding something.

During breakfast, everyone ate in silence. Callum tried to focus his attention on the scrumptious meal, but he had a one-track mind. If the Gillcrests were trying to conceal something about their other children, why would they keep their sketches on the wall? It seemed to him that they'd have gotten rid of all of the evidence. Those pictures were practically begging folks to ask questions.

Callum could hardly take his eyes off the sketches the entire time he ate. Perhaps he could do some digging after breakfast.

As soon as the lad cleared the table, he excused himself and headed toward his cabin. The smoked Irish slave he had a run-in with out in the field followed him out the door and stopped him on the way back to his place. "We hold a church meeting behind the slave shacks every Sunday at nine am. You're welcome to join us."

Callum had never been to a church service and had not dreamed it possible while serving as a slave. "I'll be there," he agreed. "My name's Callum, by the way."

The man turned away and began walking off, mumbling, "I'm aware of your name, white nigger. We will see you at nine am."

"Wait," Callum stopped him. "What's your name, if you don't mind me asking?"

The man turned and gave the lad a playful smile, "If you show up for church, I'll tell you my name there. Otherwise, forget it."

Callum was disappointed. Why would he want to attend church with people who were so miserable? What the lad needed was someone to buddy up with. Not someone who would only be nice to him if he did what they wanted him to.

Regardless of what he had said, Callum skipped the service to explore the plantation. After all, even though he had been kidnapped and forced into slavery, he was still a lad. He had heard about the colonies his whole life, yet no one in his family had ever been there. That is unless traders brought his siblings and/or parents over on another ship.

With no particular plan in mind, Callum aimlessly wandered in the opposite direction of the fields he had already grown accustomed to working. That was territory he had been curious about but hadn't had an opportunity to see.

Along the way, the lad took advantage of his alone time to think and make the most of this new land he was forced to call home. A few minutes into his walk, he found a large puddle. At first, he sloshed his way through, but after looking around to make sure nobody was watching, he sat down in it. It was cold, but in the heat of the day, it was somewhat refreshing. With the puddle being so shallow, the lad laid back in it and looked up at the few clouds passing overhead.

Callum could have stayed there soaking up the sun and enjoying that little spot all day, but a tiny voice inside of him kept saying, "Sunday is only so long. If you want to see more of the plantation, keep moving."

The property had much more to offer than Callum had imagined. A little further into his day of exploration, a creaking sound brought his feet to an abrupt halt. He heard it again and again. Allowing his ears to guide him, the lad soon found out it was nothing more than the trees cracking as they swayed in the wind. He sure hoped that noise didn't mean they were about to fall or that any of their limbs were about to crash down on him. Looking up, he caught sight of a grey squirrel jumping from one tree branch to another. Callum smiled, thrilled to see such a thing with his own eyes.

Continuing up the trail, Callum came to a fast-moving stream. Still damp from the puddle and able to clearly see the bottom, he stepped in. The stream was a bit deeper than he realized, coming up to just above his knees. The lad took a few more steps, only to stumble into a much deeper part. Standing on his tip-toes, the water still touched his chin. Callum backed out slowly and began walking along the water's edge, looking for an easier way to cross. About ten minutes upstream, he found what he was looking for — a narrow log crossing the creek. Cautiously, the lad stepped on it and took a few steps over the water.

Shaking, yet refusing to retreat, the lad sat on the log, with one leg dangling off each side. Putting both hands in front of him, he pushed himself up and scooted forward a couple of inches. He repeated the process many times over until safely arriving on the other side.

Once on dry ground, he turned back to face the log. "Don't be offended if I find a different way to return home," he apologized before continuing his journey.

Nearly an hour into his walk, Callum stumbled upon something that didn't fit well with the surroundings — half a dozen mounds of dirt covered with large stones. They resembled burial plots of family pets from back home. But if that's what they were, somebody sure had lost a lot of pets. Perhaps there was another explanation. Maybe they were graves, but they weren't for animals. But nobody buries that many folks so far away from houses. Then again, Callum wasn't in Ireland anymore, and people in the colonies had odd ways of doing things. As strange as the Gillcrests were, Callum doubted even they would want to drag bodies that far to bury them. But if those mounds weren't graves, what could they be?

One thing was for sure, he wouldn't tell a soul about his discovery. Instead, he'd make a mental note of where they were in case he decided to explore further at another time.

CHAPTER ELEVEN

LIGHTNING

As soon as breakfast was over, Master Cyrus ordered Callum to hitch up the horse. "Throw an ax in the back of the wagon and then drive it to the southernmost part of the field. A tree's been down over there for a couple of weeks. Chop it up, and have it back here by lunch."

Drive the horse and cart? Now that sounded fun! Sure, Callum had ridden a horse before. But he'd never gotten to drive a carriage. "Yes, sir. I'll get right on it."

"Have you hitched up a wagon before?" Master Josiah interjected.

The last thing Callum wanted was to miss out on such an opportunity. So, he did what came naturally to him; he lied. "Yes, sir. I know what I'm doing."

Rushing to the barn, the lad untethered Lightning. "Come with me, girl. We've got work to do," he said, holding onto Lightning's halter and leading her to the wagon.

In no time, he had her hitched. Hopping onto the seat, Callum felt like a grown-up. "We're going to have ourselves a good time," he told his four-legged coworker. Lightning whinnied with perfect timing, as though she were excited about the ride. Callum grinned.

Slightly lifting the reins as he'd seen others do, the lad gently brought them down to connect with her back. "Getty-up, Lightning."

That silly horse didn't move a muscle. Callum tried again, this time with slightly more effort. Lightning let out another whinny.

"Come on, girl cut me some slack. I don't know what I'm doing here," Callum pleaded. Raising the reins, he brought them down hard, "Getty-up!"

Lightning darted into the field much faster than Callum had anticipated. No wonder they named her Lightning!

"Slow down, girl," he panicked, hitting her with the reins again. Lightning bucked and neighed, knocking the wagon off balance.

Remembering what he had seen before, Callum pulled back on the reins, "Whoa, girl!"

It worked! The horse came to a complete stop.

Master Josiah and Master Cyrus ran from the backside of the plantation house. "What's going on here?" Master Josiah shouted. "That's no way to treat a horse! Get down out of there at once!"

Master Josiah and Master Cyrus circled the wagon, examining the wheels and Lightning. "Father," Master Cyrus said, rubbing his hand along Lightning's lower front leg, "Look at this."

Nervously, Callum followed Master Josiah from a short distance. Master Josiah rubbed the horse's leg as well. His hand stopped a little below her knee. Making eye contact with Master Cyrus, he said, "It's warm and swollen. You know what that means, right, son?"

"Yes, sir. She's hurt a ligament."

Callum felt horrible. As much as he loved animals, he couldn't believe he had done something to hurt one so recklessly. "I'm sorry," he said. "I didn't mean to."

"It doesn't matter what you *meant* to do," Master Cyrus snapped. "You *did* hurt her. And now we're stuck with a lame horse. If we don't put her down, it could take her nine months or longer to heal up enough to work."

Callum cried. Had he told the truth, somebody may have shown him how to drive the cart, and none of this would have happened. Not that anything could be done about it now. "Please don't put her down," the lad pleaded. "I'll take care of her 'til she's better."

Master Josiah gave his son a questioning look.

"I think we should put her down, Father. We can get another horse that we can use right away. Ole Lightning has done us well over the years, but feedin' her for the next nine months when she's no use to us isn't worth it. Besides, having the red-leg put her down might teach him a lesson."

Callum's lower lip jutted out as his eyes pleaded with Master Josiah. It would be bad enough if Lightning had to die because of his error, but it would be far worse if he were the one ending her life.

"I'm sorry, Callum. But my son here is right. It's the best way."

Callum broke into a cold sweat. The few tears trickling down his cheeks turned into full-fledged sobbing. It wasn't Lightning's fault. Why did she have to pay the price for something she had no control over?

Master Cyrus unhooked the horse. Glaring at Callum, he said, "This way, *crybaby*!"

Wiping his face with his forearm, Callum followed Master Cyrus and Lightning back to the plantation house. As they approached the house, Master Cyrus handed Callum the reins. Hold onto her. I'll be right back."

As the lad watched Master Cyrus enter the house, he turned to face Lightning. "Sorry, girl. I don't know what to do. I'd like to set you free, but if I do, they'll kill me and come after you anyway."

Callum stroked her mane while more tears rolled down his cheeks. "You understand, don't you, girl? You know I'm not doing this by choice, right?"

It seemed like an eternity, but eventually Master Cyrus stepped back outside, carrying a musket. Callum shook his head.

"It's okay, crybaby," Master Cyrus said. "This will all be over before you know it."

Somehow the lad doubted that. "Lead her out behind the toolshed," Master Cyrus ordered.

Callum swallowed hard. He didn't know if he could go through with this. How could he? He'd rather use that musket on Master Cyrus than on Lightning. But that was his emotions trying to take over again.

"Now!" Master Cyrus demanded, nodding his head toward the shed.

"Yes, sir," Callum said, gently pulling on Lightning's reins.

Lightning was more cooperative than Callum had hoped for. "It's amazing what dishonesty can do, isn't it?" Master Cyrus asked as they walked. "It can get a person into or out of trouble. It can keep a person alive, or in this case, cost an animal its life."

Callum sniffled, "Isn't there another way?"

"Nope. Has to be done," Master Cyrus insisted. "I need you to tie her to the fence post."

Callum shook his head.

"Do it unless you want to suffer the same fate as the horse!"

Callum's whole body trembled. If only there were a way to get out of this!

CHAPTER TWELVE

RELIVING IT

Shooting a lame horse was the hardest thing Callum had ever done. And he hated both Master Josiah and Master Cyrus for forcing him to murder her in cold blood.

The only thing more difficult than killing an innocent animal who didn't deserve to die was digging her grave. "I don't care if you have to shovel all night," Master Cyrus said. "You *will* get this horse in the ground with at least three feet of dirt on top of her before you go to bed tonight."

Callum had made many foolish mistakes in life, but never one that resulted in death. Not that his actions truly led to the horse being shot.

That was all Master Cyrus's and Master Josiah's doing. Callum couldn't forget that. He would not subject himself to accepting responsibility for Lightning's death.

"Hurry up!" Master Cyrus ordered. "The longer you make me stay out here, the more upset I'm going to get. And you don't want me to be upset!"

Now that was something Callum could agree with, though he didn't say as much. "Yes, sir. I'll work harder."

After three grueling hours of digging, Callum laid the shovel down. "Is it deep enough now?"

Master Cyrus laughed sarcastically, "Deep enough to bury you, maybe. But not a horse. You've gotta go much deeper than that. A lot wider too."

Had Master Cyrus not already taught him better, Callum would have sighed, rolled his eyes, or both. Or, at the very least, shot him an evil eye. As difficult as it was, the lad kept a straight face as he picked up his shovel and resumed digging for the umpteenth time.

"While you're workin', red-leg, I'm gonna decide if this is punishment enough or if you deserve a dozen lashes on top of it."

Callum cringed. Master Cyrus had a one-track mind – brutality.

"I'll base my decision on how you respond to my questions. Here's the first one. Did you or did you not lie to my father about knowing how to drive a horse and wagon?"

Knowing when to lie and when not to can be a daunting task. Callum wiped his sweaty hands on his breeches.

"Answer me, red-leg. Don't stand there cookin' up some big lie. Prior to today, had you ever driven a horse and wagon?"

Sinking the shovel into the ground, Callum said, "No, sir. I hadn't. I did lie to your father, and I'm sorry." He hoped that was the answer the planter's son was looking for.

"That was an easy one since it was already obvious you had no idea what you were doin'. Now, why, red-leg? Why did you lie?"

Why would he have told the truth? That would have been the better question. Callum hated being on the hot seat. Still, he had to answer if he didn't want to get backhanded or have his flesh torn open. "I thought I could handle it, and I was afraid I wouldn't get the chance to drive if I told the truth."

Master Cyrus squatted down and placed his fists on the ground for balance while peering into the lad's baby blue eyes. "That was a stupid move, red-leg. I've got just a couple more questions for ya, and then I'll make my decision. How'd it feel shootin' ole Lightning?"

Callum glanced up at the dead mare, not knowing if he could even put his feelings into words. Resting the shovel on his foot, he said, "Horrible."

"One-word answers are unacceptable. Try again, red-leg."

Why did Master Cyrus have to be so difficult? He had undoubtedly seen how upset Callum was when he squeezed that trigger. Forcing him to relive the experience was a nasty thing to do. "You're not doin' yourself any favors by not comin' out with it," Master Cyrus barked. "How did it feel?"

Oh, those stupid tears! When would Callum ever learn to control them? Blubbering, he said, "It... was... the worst thing... I've ever... had... to do." Sniffling a couple of times, the lad continued, "I didn't try to hurt her. Honest... I didn't."

Master Cyrus snickered, "You know what I like about you, red-leg?"

Callum hung his head. "That you're allowed to whip me?"

"Well, that too," Master Cyrus laughed, "But I was thinkin' more along the lines of how easy it is to get you upset. You're the whiniest lad on this plantation."

CHAPTER THIRTEEN
NO WAY

—— *ele* ——

Darcy always said blessings disguise themselves as difficulties. Perhaps she was right!

For two and a half hours Callum had tossed back and forth, unable to catch a wink of sleep. Hoping the cool night air would help, he stepped outside and laid on the ground, with his back tight against his shack. The lad hadn't been there long when the front door to the plantation house opened.

Startled, Callum watched in silence and, through squinted eyes, soon figured out it was the planter's son. At first, the lad assumed Master Cyrus was making a late-night run to the outhouse. But he wouldn't be carrying a non-lit lantern if that were the case. And why was he creeping around on his tip-toes?

Callum laid still, hoping to remain unseen. Thankfully, whatever Master Cyrus was up to, he was so focused on sneaking away from the plantation house that the last thing he was looking for was a white slave.

What could possibly be so important that the planter's son would venture out under the cover of darkness? Callum didn't take his eyes off of him.

Once Master Cyrus was far from the house, he lit the lantern. If he were meeting someone, he might talk to them about whether or not Callum was truly purchased to be his first slave. Even if that conversation never came up, Callum had to know what was going on. Ever so quietly, he stood and followed him across the field.

Master Cyrus walked at such a brisk pace that Callum struggled to keep up. Every now and then, he whipped out that old pocket watch of his, took a peek at it, and stuffed it back in his pocket.

Callum stepped on a stick, and it cracked beneath his feet. Master Cyrus stopped walking and slowly turned to look behind him. Callum plopped onto his belly and covered his head, hoping the light from the lantern wouldn't be enough to give him away. Oh, how he hoped he hadn't gotten too close!

For what seemed like an eternity, Callum lay there anxiously listening for footsteps. Not picking up a sound, ever-so-slowly he raised his head. Master Cyrus and the lantern were gone. Not knowing whether Master Cyrus had gone ahead or simply blown out the lantern to hide from him, Callum was at a loss.

If the planter's son was in hiding, as soon as the lad stood up, he would be busted. If, however, Master Cyrus was moving ahead and Callum didn't get up soon, he might never catch up. How did the lad get himself into such predicaments?

Stealthily, Callum rose to his feet. Hoping he made the right decision, the lad took a giant step forward. If Master Cyrus were watching, he didn't come out of hiding. Eyeing the ground closely in an effort to avoid making any more noise, Callum took three more giant steps and stopped. Not seeing any sign of light or hearing anything out of the ordinary, he convinced himself he had been left behind.

Breaking into a slow jog, Callum headed in the direction he had last seen Master Cyrus walking in. For ten minutes or so, he ran in the dark before catching sight of the lantern. Master Cyrus was still walking at a brisk pace. Callum slowed to match his speed. This time, he would stay far enough behind that he could barely even see the light.

Half an hour later, Callum saw more lights ahead. Master Cyrus was meeting somebody, alright. Perhaps it was multiple somebodies. The more eyes there were, the more dangerous his spying would become. Regardless, if Callum wanted to know what was happening, he would have to be close enough to see and hear what was taking place.

"There he is," a male voice rang out. "We were starting to think you weren't coming! Where's Lightning?"

"Sorry," Master Cyrus called out. "I ran her a bit too hard the other night, and she tore a ligament."

What? Surely Callum hadn't heard that right. What did Master Cyrus mean *he* ran her too hard? The lad followed at a faster pace until he got within a few yards of the clearing where Master Cyrus had joined several others.

"Sorry about the horse," one of his friends said. "I know our game went a little longer than normal the last time we played. Did you make it back home before your old man caught you?"

"Oh, yeah!" Master Cyrus bragged. "He didn't suspect a thing. I even set things up so the new red-leg took the fall for injuring the horse!"

Callum couldn't believe his ears. Here he thought Lightning died because of his error, as did everyone else on the plantation. The lad had lost much sleep and shed many tears over his own guilt, even though he had desperately tried to convince himself it wasn't his fault. It turned out he had been right the whole time.

"What about my payment?" Another fellow asked. "I beat you fair and square."

"I know," Master Cyrus said, pulling a medium-sized knife and a shepherd's sling from his pockets. "And I'm payin' up. I brought a couple of options for you. You can choose one, and then I'll use the other as a wager for tonight's game."

Gambling? That's what they were doing! Master Gillcrest and Mistress Rosanna would not approve.

Master Cyrus's friend chose the shepherd's sling. It was one of the finest Callum had ever seen. He sure wished he could have shot or at least held it once before Master Cyrus gave it away to strangers.

Callum's mind returned to Lightning as he watched the guys setting up their game. That had to have been the dirtiest move the lad had ever heard of. The planter's son must have been born without a conscience!

Chapter Fourteen

THE FEUD

On his way to the plantation house, Callum overheard the feud of the century.

"I'm sorry," Mistress Rosanna shouted. "I'm sorry for not living up to your expectations! Believe it or not, I am a human being and am not perfect!"

"You can say that again!" Master Josiah yelled back at her. "Do you know how hard it is to be married to you? You snore so loud a man can't get a wink of sleep, you hog both sides of the bed, half the time you burn our meals, you stay behind on the laundry, you—"

Master Cyrus jumped in, "Stop talkin' to her that way. She doesn't deserve that, and you know it!"

"Who do you think you are?" Master Josiah shouted at him. "I won't hesitate to tan your hide if you dare speak to me in that tone of voice again!"

"You'll do no such thing," Mistress Rosanna fired back. "You're not going to discourage my baby from standing up for a woman, especially his mother!"

Callum wasn't about to enter the plantation house with all that drama going on. Freezing in his tracks, he wondered what started such a quarrel. If it went on long enough, he was sure to find out.

Mistress Rosanna turned her attention back to Master Josiah, "Surely you don't think you're the kind of man every woman dreams of marrying! Throwin' your clothes around all over the house, never lifting a finger to help me in the kitchen but still expecting me to help with the outside chores, always fussin' at me or Cyrus over practically nothing, not to mention how rare it is that you clean yourself up. What's it been, four months since you last bathed? And I'm sure I don't have to mention how your violent temper destroyed our entire family!"

"That's enough, woman!" Master Josiah shouted. "You are way out of line!"

Master Cyrus butted in again, "She's not the one out of line. You are!"

Callum was thankful he was outside, even though he wished he could find a safe place to witness what was taking place in there. It sounded like one of the Gillcrests got thrown across the kitchen table. There were a lot of thuds and smacks, and in no time, Master Cyrus shot out of the house with his father chasing after him.

By now, other slaves were joining Callum. Together, they stood twenty feet or so from the plantation house, none daring to enter. Master Cyrus bolted toward the barn, with Master Josiah hot on his trail. They ran a complete lap around the toolshed and disappeared into a wooded area.

The slaves exchanged suspicious glances with one another, but none spoke. Whatever was going on between the Gillcrests would likely stay between the Gillcrests regardless of how much Callum yearned for more information.

Mistress Rosanna stepped onto the porch and, in a voice as sweet as molasses, called,

"Supper's ready. You all need to get to that table and start filling your bellies. There's a lot of work to do today."

Callum made eye contact with one of the Smoked Irish, who nodded toward the house. Callum thought about returning the nod. Why should he go first? The Smoked Irish slave was older and had undoubtedly been there longer. But what good would come of arguing? Hesitantly, Callum started toward the house.

Behind him, a couple of slaves were whispering. One of them said, "I bet Master Josiah's glad Master Oliver's not still around with that ole sling. Remember what he did that time when—"

"You know we ain't supposed to talk 'bout that," another replied.

Callum hated it when people said just enough to pique his interest before stalling a conversation. Now not only did he have to wonder what Mistress Rosanna was talking about minutes before, but now he had to find out who this Master Oliver was and what he did with a sling.

Inside, Callum plopped down next to the other slaves, all of which remained silent. Mistress Rosanna, on the other hand, hummed up a storm with a smile on her face as she set food on the table. Her happiness was as fake as the welcoming grin of a crocodile, but at least she attempted to lighten the mood.

It didn't work. Master Cyrus let out a yelp from somewhere outside. Master Josiah hollered, "Keep those hands out of the way!"

Callum couldn't hear any lashes, but Master Josiah must have followed through on his threat because his son was hollering out in pain while pleading for mercy, "Stop! That's too hard! Stop! That's enough already! Ow! Ow! It won't happen again! Please!"

Mistress Rosanna increased the volume of her humming while literally stomping across the floor to get a pail of water, which she persisted to slam on the table, still smiling as if she didn't have a care in the world.

Chapter Fifteen

BLACKMAIL

Master Cyrus was in a foul mood, likely due to the correction he'd received from his father. Shoving Callum from behind, he knocked the lad to the ground. "Keep out of my way next time, red-leg."

Callum stood and dusted off his shirt and breeches. Even though he had every right to be angry, he wasn't. He understood why Master Cyrus had stood up for his mother and didn't think it was fair that he had been beaten for doing it. That would be enough to upset anybody. Maybe ole Master Cyrus needed someone to help him lift his spirits. Picking the hoe back up, Callum said, "Master

Cyrus, I was wondering. How do you gamble? You know, like with playing cards?"

Master Cyrus's arms tensed, and both eyebrows raised. "What makes you think I know how to gamble?"

Callum shook his head, "No reason. Just wondering if you knew."

Master Cyrus looked around before stepping closer to the lad. "You're lyin', red-leg. You asked for a reason. Tell it to me straight, or I'm gonna whip you good!"

Callum and that big mouth of his! Someday he might learn to bite his tongue, but he hadn't quite gotten there yet. "I figured since you go out and play against your friends at night, you might be able to teach me."

Master Cyrus backhanded the lad. "You don't know what you're talkin' about, red-leg. And you better not repeat this nonsense to anybody. Got it?"

Callum rubbed his lip. Sure enough, it was bleeding. By now, he'd been hit enough times that the pain was barely noticeable. Perhaps he could share just one more jab. "Don't worry," he said. "I won't *tell* anybody what you've been doing."

"What's that supposed to mean?" Master Cyrus scoffed.

"It means I won't *tell* anybody what I know, but it sure would be a crying shame if you're out one night and something happens to wake your folks up. Wonder what would happen if they find your room empty one night when you're supposed to be sleeping in it?"

"You tell anybody anything about me, and you won't live to regret it."

"Do you think I care about whether I live or die? What do I have to live for? To be a slave for the rest of my life? Let me make you a promise too. If you don't quit backhanding and threatening me with that whip all the time, I'll make sure your folks find out not only that you've been sneaking out to gamble but about what *you* did to the horse too."

Master Cyrus took a step back. "If my father hadn't purchased you to be my first slave, I'd kill you right now. But I'd rather wait until you're mine so I can beat you to a bloody pulp, with or without a cause, and believe me when I say I will thoroughly enjoy every minute of your screamin' before putting you in the ground. You don't know who you're messin' with, red-leg."

Callum smirked. Whether the planter's son would admit it or not, Callum had the upper hand. "Don't forget what I said," he told him.

"You keep bullying me, and rest assured, when the timing's right, your parents will find out what you've been doing behind their backs."

Master Cyrus glared at Callum for two minutes before turning and walking away. If Callum read him right, Master Cyrus wasn't going to challenge him. Victory! What a sweet smell!

Chapter Sixteen

Mystery Box

Callum had never seen that before. Either it hadn't been there, or he was blinder than a bat. There was no way he had missed that small wooden crate, partially covered by rocks sitting just inside the toolshed door.

Curious, Callum swept the rocks off the top and lifted the lid. What a random assortment of items! An oddly familiar-looking doll made from corn husks, a couple of pocket knives, a ball, a hair ribbon, a necklace, and *wait!* Was that medium-sized knife the same one Callum had seen at the card game? It had been dark, but it sure looked similar. But if it was, how did it end up in a partially-covered box?

A chill crept down Callum's spine. How could the items in that crate possibly be related to one another? If it weren't for the knife, the lad could have convinced himself the chest had been there since long before he arrived in the colonies, and somehow, he'd just been overlooking it. But he was near certain that was the same knife Master Cyrus had offered to a fellow gambler. If he was right about that, Master Cyrus must have returned the knife to that box after the game. But if that were the case, it didn't make sense why the crate was covered with rocks. The numbers simply weren't adding up.

Gently closing the lid, the lad placed the rocks back on top of the crate, making it appear exactly as it had before he'd touched it. Afraid of getting caught, Callum decided he'd better get out of there fast. Unfortunately, Master Cyrus was passing by on his way to the outhouse as the lad exited the toolshed. "What are you snoopin' around for, red-leg?"

"I was putting the tools away, sir."

"That better be all you were doin', or I'll—" Master Cyrus stopped speaking midsentence and continued his trail to the outhouse.

Yes indeed. Callum's plan had worked! Master Cyrus, at least for the time being, was finished with the threats and terror tactics.

Callum closed the toolshed and slowly made his way back to the plantation house. While admiring the gorgeous sunset, he couldn't help but wonder how much longer his peace with the planter's son could last.

Kicking something, Callum stopped and looked down. It was a turtle. Oh, how he loved those things! Squatting, Callum said, "Hey, little guy. Where you headed?" The lad probably would have screamed at the top of his lungs if the critter had answered. Since he didn't, Callum picked him up, and the little guy tucked his head back inside the shell. Even so, the turtle was one of the friendlier types. He didn't close his cover completely, so Callum could still see his orangish-brown eyes.

"You're adorable," Callum told him. "I bet you have no idea how good you've got it. Anytime you want to, you can just shut yourself inside, and nobody can mess with you. You don't have to be anybody's slave. I'd trade places with you any day."

Callum looked over his shoulder. Still no sign of Master Cyrus or anybody else. "Would you mind if I keep you for a pet? I sure could use the company."

The outhouse door slammed. "Hey, what do you have there?" Master Cyrus called.

Callum spun around and proudly held the little guy out in front of him, "I found a turtle!"

"I see that," Master Cyrus said, hurriedly approaching. Drawing closer, he held his palm out, "Let me see it, red-leg."

Callum didn't want to. Master Cyrus might make him get rid of the little guy. One of the many harsh realities of being a slave was not getting to make decisions for himself. As much as the lad didn't want to, he handed the turtle over.

Master Cyrus started to peek inside the shell as Callum had, but as soon as he brought the turtle to eye level, the little guy closed his cover and hissed.

"Wanna play favorites, do you?" Master Cyrus asked, slamming it on the ground. "Looks like turtle stew for dessert!"

"No!" Callum yelled. "I won't let you!"

"*You* won't *let me*, huh?" Master Cyrus laughed. "We'll see about that."

"Is that a *gamble* you're willing to take?" Callum asked, squinting his eyes and gritting his teeth in anticipation of getting backhanded.

Master Cyrus glared at him. "I don't appreciate your attitude," he said. "The last guy that talked to me like—"

Callum cut him off, "Sorry we're late, Master Josiah!" he called.

"Nice try," Master Cyrus continued without looking behind him, "The last guy who—"

"You lads are late for supper," Master Josiah called, sounding angry.

Master Cyrus kicked the turtle so hard it flew at least ten feet into the air. "Sorry, sir," he said. "We're on our way."

CHAPTER SEVENTEEN

A LITTLE MORE DIGGING

Two months had passed since Callum's middle-of-nowhere discovery. Since then, he had privately asked each of the Gillcrests about the dirt mounds. According to Master Josiah, nothing about that part of the land had changed since his grandparents bought the property forty or fifty years before. He claimed there was no way of telling what was under that dirt and that nobody on the plantation had ever had time to investigate. Mistress Rosanna asserted she had never been to that side of the plantation and had never heard of mounds of any kind anywhere on the property. Master Cyrus said his grandparents used to keep cattle back there, and when their animals died of illnesses, they buried them all in the same area.

It had taken Callum long enough to build up his nerve, but it was time to uncover the truth. The twelve-year-old couldn't have asked for a more perfect night. Not only was Master Cyrus out gambling with his buddies, but the full moon was so bright it felt as if the day had already broken.

Breathing hard, Callum dragged the last heavy stone off the first mound. Returning to an upright position, he picked up the shovel and dug in. Removing the first scoop of earth filled the lad with excitement. By the time he got to the tenth shovel full, his anticipation had evolved into fear.

Fifteen minutes into his furious digging spree, the shovel smacked into something that was neither soil nor rock. Tossing the shovel, Callum dropped to his hands and knees and began gently sweeping the object with his bare hands. In no time, he had no doubt he had uncovered bone, human or animal he didn't know. For the fiftieth time since beginning his search, Callum glanced over his shoulder. Thankfully, no one was watching.

Terrified beyond imagination, Callum continued cleaning off the bone. Through twenty minutes of concentrated effort, he finally got it to a place where it was positively identifiable — he was looking at the remains of a human foot. Not knowing how many other bones might be in that mound, the lad continued excavating and had an entire leg uncovered within an hour. Stopping was not an option, but taking a break was unavoidable.

Callum lay on his side, using one of his arms as a pillow. The lad's discovery left him with more questions than answers. Whose leg was he looking at? How did the person die? How long had he or she been buried? Did the Gillcrests know at least one of those burial mounds contained human bones? Most importantly, how could he find the answers he was looking for?

The lad closed his eyes for a moment. He replayed Master Cyrus's story in his head. Master Cyrus never wanted to tell Callum anything. Why would he have so freely shared information about the plantation land's history? Because it wasn't true, that's why! Finding the bones of a human leg in one of the mounds clearly proved that. But why would the planter's son make up such a tale? Probably for the same reason he made up the idea that Callum would one day be his first official slave. Callum didn't believe that story any more than he believed this one. Master Cyrus was the most dishonest person he'd ever met.

Callum's body suddenly jerked. He knew what that meant. If he lay there any longer, he was going to fall asleep. There was no time for that. He had to get back to work.

It took many long hours, but Callum unearthed an intact full-body skeleton of someone who had either died young or had lived his life as a little person. If Callum had to guess, he'd say that body probably belonged to the child of a slave. For whatever reason, the Gillcrests didn't want anybody to know about it. But what sense would that make? If they owned the slaves, they couldn't get in trouble if one of them died. He didn't think so anyway.

Now there was a bigger question, one Callum wished he hadn't thought of. He had only uncovered one mound. What about the others? What if each mound contained the body of another slave child? Then again, what if they didn't? Perhaps only one or two were human skeletons, and the rest were livestock graves.

Staring at the bones in front of him, Callum knew the only way to remove all shadow of doubt was to dig up every mound. Doing so was out of the question. He had already disrespected the dead. Repeating the offense time and again would be a heinous act for which he could never forgive himself. But how could the lad walk away without fully solving the mystery when the evidence was right there in front of him? People could have been murdered. And with all of the contradictions in the Gillcrests' stories, that was a strong possibility.

Callum chewed on his bottom lip. Even if the graves belonged to murder victims, digging up their remains wouldn't undo their deaths. What good would it do?

The longer the lad remained in the woods, the better the chances he would get caught. And hoeing tobacco plants all day with no sleep is not something he looked forward to.

That settled it. Scooting to the other side of the skeleton, Callum began kicking dirt atop the remains. Returning to his quarters was the only logical option.

By the time Callum finished, the mound, as best as he could tell in the moonlight, looked the same as it had before he had dug it up. Dusting himself off, the lad headed back toward his shack, stopping only when something darted behind a tree, causing his heart to nearly jump out of his chest.

"Hello?" Callum called softly.

There was no answer.

Callum wasn't sure if that made the situation better or worse. Hopefully, it was nothing. He took a few steps, then abruptly stopped in his tracks. Hearing no footsteps had to be a good sign. Unless, of course, it meant whatever darted behind that tree wasn't a living thing. He had heard talk of evil spirits. What if he had woken one up at the graveyard? What if he had unleashed something that would terrorize him for the rest of his days?

Callum took a few more steps and stopped again, still not hearing or seeing a thing. It wasn't the safe kind of silence; it was the weird kind. Why had he been so foolish?

Dropping the shovel, the lad raced toward his shack, looking over his shoulder every few yards. By the time he got to the stream, he was panting like a dog. Oh, how he wanted to stop long enough to soothe his throat with some of that cool water. But there wasn't time! Whoever or whatever was out there with him could be closing in.

Not caring how wet he got or how cold the water was, Callum jumped in. Unfortunately, he forgot some parts of the stream were deeper than others. This time, he went completely underwater and couldn't touch the bottom. As soon as his head popped up, he hollered, "Help!"

The stream carried Callum and forced his body to slam into rock after rock.

The next thing the lad knew, his eyes were popping open, and he was lying atop the grave he had filled in shortly before. It wasn't a nightmare. Callum was drenched from head to toe. How he got there, he didn't know, nor did he want to find out.

Scared out of his mind, the preteen once again made a mad dash for home, this time determined to be more careful. Even though he was moving swiftly, he'd have to watch his every step. Whoever or whatever was out there, wanted to toy with him, and he couldn't let it happen. Too bad nobody told that tree root that! Callum tripped over it and fell flat on his face. Jumping back to his feet, not even looking behind him, he tried to run but was so off balance from the previous fall that he went down a second time.

"Calm down, Callum," he whispered to himself. "Use your noggin."

The lad stood back to his feet, looked around for a second, took a deep breath, and instead of sprinting, began jogging toward his cabin. It took a while, but eventually Callum's place came into view. Hoping he had outrun his unseen enemy and that no one on the plantation would see him, the lad picked up his pace. When he got to his cabin, he jetted inside, slammed the door behind him, and lugged his bed in front of it.

Bringing his hand to his chest, Callum feared his heart might explode. He hadn't run that far or that fast ever in his life. Leaning his back against a wall, the lad attempted to slow his breathing. After ten minutes of keeping still, he laid on his bed, fully aware that sleep would be an improbability, regardless of how badly his eyelids burned.

Working without pay and being referred to as a red-leg, a white nigger, and a poor-white earth scratching scum, getting smacked around and constantly threatened with whippings was taking its toll. Not to mention the frequent nightmares the lad had that one day he would really become the property of Master Cyrus.

There had to be something better to think about than graves, murders, and evil spirits. But what? Freedom! That was it. How had he forgotten about Uncle Keir? Perhaps it wasn't an evil spirit he'd been running from. Maybe Uncle Keir had come to the colonies searching for him? But if so, why didn't he rescue him yet? Perhaps he was waiting for just the right moment.

Why was he kidding himself? If Uncle Keir were going to rescue him, he'd have done it back in Dublin. The only way he would gain freedom would be if he got it for himself. And he would! Just as soon as he figured out the route back to Dublin, or at least thought of a way to escape the plantation without getting caught.

The lad couldn't help but wonder if he might have a better chance of getting away with it if he could form a league with the other slaves. Perhaps, just perhaps, Callum could force himself to attend one of those Sunday services the other slaves held. Maybe they would give him a chance to speak, and together they could develop a plan to attain their independence.

CHAPTER EIGHTEEN

THE

PREDICAMENT

The fire in Master Josiah's eyes blazed hotter than Callum had ever seen them. Stomping his foot and chopping through an imaginary spider web with both arms, he shouted, "Where is it, son? Stop carrying off my tools! Especially ones I inherited from my father!"

"I don't know where it is," Master Cyrus insisted, retreating a few steps. I promise I haven't touched it in weeks."

The planter stormed closer until his nose nearly touched Master Cyrus's. "Shovels don't have legs, son! It didn't up and walk away on its own!"

The shovel? That's what they were fighting about? Callum couldn't reveal its whereabouts; Darcy always said it was wrong to involve oneself in the disputes of others.

"Ten minutes, Cyrus!" Master Josiah snapped. "You find that shovel and place it in my hand within the next ten minutes, or we're going to have a contest to see which gets wore out first — my belt or your backside."

Thankful he wasn't the one getting a verbal thrashing, Callum swallowed hard as the planter's son ran toward the toolshed. He sure hoped Master Cyrus's search wouldn't lead him anywhere near the graveyard.

Pretending to be so focused on his work that he didn't see or hear anything, Callum continued the never-ending job of hoeing the field. If that shovel were to be found, he would have much explaining to do. At least there was plenty of time to come up with a good story.

Callum could say he had no idea how it got out there. But that would never work since he had already questioned so many people about the dirt mounds. He'd have to come up with something better than that. Maybe he could run with that evil spirit thing. He could tell them a demonic force had been haunting him ever since he had visited that area of land, and he was trying to appease the spirit by taking him a gift? Who ever heard of giving a gift to an evil spirit? Maybe they'd believe him if he said that's how they did things in Ireland?

The gruff-voiced smoked Irish slave suddenly appeared out of nowhere. "You better hope they don't find out," he growled.

If Callum had ever met anyone who creeped him out, it was that man. Playing stupid, the lad asked, "What are you talking about?"

Shaking his head, the man chuckled and walked away.

"What are you talking about?" Callum repeated, louder than before.

The man continued on his way as if Callum hadn't uttered a word.

Somehow the smoked Irish slave knew. Callum wondered if the man had been watching him the night before. But how could he have been? Callum had waited until late in the night when everybody would have been asleep before creeping out of his cabin. But how else could that man know anything lest he had been out there? Surely, he didn't communicate with the spirit world!

Callum had to learn more about the peculiar man. On Sunday, if he didn't leave the plantation before then, the lad planned to attend the slaves' church service. And he was going to find out just how much that man knew.

Suddenly overcome with an uncanny feeling somebody was watching him, Callum dropped the hoe and scanned his surroundings. Somebody's eyes were zeroing in on him. He couldn't see them, but they were there.

Uncomfortable but unable to do anything about it, Callum reached for his hoe, only to find a green snake slithering next to it. Of all things to be watching him! Callum detested snakes. So much, as a matter of fact, he ran several steps backward, tripping over his own two feet. Jumping up, he found himself next to a thin pine tree with low enough branches to enable him to scramble ten feet up it in less than two minutes.

Callum stopped to catch his breath and looked down to ensure the green snake wasn't chasing him. That's when he realized how far he had climbed. Snakes may have been his number one fear. But heights ran a close second. Panicking, Callum wrapped both arms around the tree, squeezing it with all his might.

For the first time in his life, fear caused Callum to pee himself.

Wet breeches was the least of his problems. Master Josiah was heading his way and wasn't whistling a joyous song. If the planter found him in that tree instead of working, he was going to get his first lashing. But how was a clumsy lad like him supposed to get down without falling? And in the event he safely made it to the ground, and that snake got anywhere near him, what then?

Squinting his eyes tighter than he knew was possible, the lad envisioned himself falling out of the tree where the green snake would unhinge its jaws and bite him with a set of enormous fangs, and then he pictured Master Josiah dragging him toward the whipping post. It was too much! Callum feared he was going to faint.

It took the lad a minute to find the strength, but once he opened his eyes, he was relieved to find Master Josiah had changed course and was heading toward the plantation house. Not that his leaving would make it any easier to get out of the tree. Callum's legs trembled at the thought. Closing his eyes again, the lad forced himself to take his left foot off the branch it was resting on and feel for the limb beneath it. It took some doing, but Callum managed to move his foot down a branch. Darcy always said the first step was the hardest. If that were the case, he could do this!

Even though it took no more than two minutes to get up that tree, it took at least fifteen to come back down. But the lad made it without getting as much as a splinter.

Callum had no more than started back to work when a crash of thunder rattled the very ground he stood on. Looking up, he saw dark storm clouds moving in. Maybe, just maybe, if God existed, He felt bad enough about all Callum had gone through that He'd make it rain so nobody would notice his wet breeches. It could happen!

Cloud shadows glided graciously across the tobacco crops. Gradually, the light breeze that had been blowing for the past few hours turned into a full-fledged wind. The harder it blew, the wider Callum's grin became.

A drop of water fell on his arm. "Yes, yes, yes!" the lad exclaimed. That drop turned into another, and another, and in a matter of seconds, Callum was drenched. With no one watching, Callum dropped the hoe, looked toward the sky, and opened his mouth as wide as he could. After getting his face and tongue well-watered, the lad folded his arms like they were chicken wings, flapped them up and down, and skipped around in circles while laughing out loud for the first time in nearly two years.

CHAPTER NINETEEN

THE SERVICE

Somehow the church service didn't rise to Callum's expectations. The lad had never been to church before, but he'd heard enough about services to have a picture in his mind of what one should be like, and this wasn't it.

"Look who finally decided to grace us with his presence," the gruff-voiced smoked Irish slave said as Callum approached, directing all eyes to the twelve-year-old.

Feeling like a barn cat someone had tossed into a stream, Callum said, "Thanks for inviting me."

"No need to be shy, Callum. Pull up a seat next to my wife, Amelia. I know you've seen the rest of these people. Have you had a chance to talk to any of 'em?"

Grabbing a chair and moving it next to Amelia, Callum shook his head, "No, sir."

"Sir?" the man laughed. "Sir, coming from a white nigger! Now, I like that!"

Being mocked at a church service, of all places, was not something Callum had prepared himself for. Maybe the smoked Irish slave wasn't trying to make fun of him, but it sure felt that way.

The man continued, "Let me tell you who is who. First, I should tell you my name; I'm Jonah. Again, the gorgeous creature sitting next to you is my wife, Amelia." Pausing for a moment, he gave his wife a flirtatious wink. "This lady, and her daddy, are responsible for me being the preacher I am today! She told me about the Lord and showed me how to get saved, and her daddy helped me recognize God's callin' on my life!"

Extending his hand toward an older teenager whose dagger-shooting eyes would lead one to believe she was about to swallow a live toad, Jonah said, "This is our daughter, Keziah. God blessed us with her shortly after we lost our son."

The smoked Irish slave and his wife looked at each other in silence for a moment. Moving on, the man nodded to a couple of chairs opposite where his family sat and went on with the introductions, "The other white nigger sitting over there is Ghazi. He doesn't say much to anybody. He's the kind of guy that prefers to stay to himself. Next to him is Jemimah. All I'm going to say about her is you better be careful to stay on her good side." The congregation laughed. "And next to Jemimah is Caspar, a man who just became our brother in Christ a few months ago."

Callum had undoubtedly seen all the slaves before — whether at mealtime or when they were busying about the fields. It was nice to finally have names to put with their faces.

"Caspar," Jonah said. "Go ahead and ask the Lord to bless our meeting. Would you?"

For the first time, as Caspar stood to his feet, Callum noticed a scar the middle-aged man had on his left cheek. It looked like the letter R. Callum had no way of knowing what that meant, but it didn't look like that scar was something he had gotten due to an accident.

Seeing the other slaves bow their heads, Callum followed suit.

"Dear Lord, Caspar began. "What a fine day You've given us! That sun is shining oh so brightly. Those birds are singing the sweetest of melodies. None of us are sick. You, God, are amazingly powerful! You, God, are who we want to praise! Fill us with your Holy Spirit! Let us feel you moving in our midst! Help us be strong in the faith! We pray all of this in the name of that precious son of Yours', Jesus Christ! Amen."

Prayer-poems were confusing. That one sounded nothing at all like the one Master Cyrus had used. Callum wondered how many more prayer-poems believers committed to memory.

Without breathing another word, Jemimah took a deep breath, closed her eyes, and sang a song unlike any Callum had ever heard. He found himself tapping his foot as she sang:

Ah, holy Jesus, how hast Thou offended,
That man to judge Thee hath in hate pretended?
By foes derided, by Thine own rejected,
O most afflicted.

Who was the guilty? Who brought this upon thee?
Alas, my treason, Jesus, hath undone Thee.
'Twas I, Lord, Jesus, I it was denied Thee!

I crucified Thee.

The words were beautiful. Jemimah's voice was moving. Callum felt something deep inside of him that he'd never felt before. The other slaves were singing along with her. He only wished he better understood what they were singing about. The song continued:

For me, kind Jesus, was Thy incarnation,
Thy mortal sorrow, and Thy life's oblation;
Thy death of anguish and Thy bitter passion,
For my salvation.

Therefore, kind Jesus, since I cannot pay Thee,
I do adore Thee, and will ever pray Thee,
Think on Thy pity and Thy love unswerving,
Not my deserving.

As soon as Jemimah stopped singing, Keziah sprang up, raised both arms high in the air, and trembled like a scorpion who had just gotten a bucket of ice water dumped on her. "Oh Jesus, Jesus, Jesus!" she shrieked. "Lord of my life! We love you, Jesus!"

Callum had never witnessed such a spectacle. Everybody was smiling, and a couple of them were shouting things like, "Praise the Lord," and "That's right, sister!" Between the clapping hands, the stomping feet, and streaming tears, Callum couldn't help but wonder if they had all gone mad. Suppressing the belly laugh he knew would come across as an insult to their idea of worship proved difficult. The lad was relieved when Jonah stood, and a hush fell over the small assembly, "Let me share a word from the Good Book," he said.

Glancing around, Callum didn't see any books of any kind. If he had ever wanted circumstantial evidence that there were people on earth who came from other planets, he was starting to believe he had found it.

"The Good Book says, 'I will love thee, O Lord, my strength. The Lord is my rock, and my fortress, and my deliverer; my God, my strength, in whom I will trust; my buckler, and the horn of my salvation, and my high tower. I will call upon the Lord, who is worthy to be praised: so shall I be saved from mine enemies.' Listen to me, now, children. We need to praise God when things are going well and when they're not going so well. We need to praise Him when that sun's out and even when it hides its face from us. We need to praise the Lord when we're working hard and when we're too sick to get out of bed. When our enemies try to knock us down, we need to cry for God's deliverance. He can and will do it! We have to put our trust in Him!"

"Yes, yes, yes, Jesus!" Jemimah squealed, waving both hands high above her head. "Oh, praise His dear, sweet name! Thank you, Jesus!"

Callum was beginning to understand why his parents had never allowed him to attend church. Church folks were nuts! How exactly does one go into hysterics about passages from a book they didn't have about a man named God they couldn't see, touch, or hear?

For hours, those poor, brainwashed souls sang, shouted, and bragged about how good God was. Sometimes they laughed; sometimes they cried. Callum didn't understand but about half of their nonsense, but he couldn't deny he was enjoying himself at least a little.

When things finally settled down, Jonah took Callum aside. "You didn't come here to learn about God, did you, lad?"

By reflexive instinct, Callum opened his mouth to lie, but something caused him to bite his tongue. It was as though he couldn't speak anything but the truth. "No, sir."

Jonah placed his hand on top of Callum's head, "I told you before," he said firmly. "Stop thinking that way."

Callum felt a tingling sensation in both cheeks, "Stop thinking *what* way?"

"Stop dreaming of running off, lad. Nobody here is going to help you get yourself hurt. The Gillcrests aren't that bad of people. We've got it better than some."

Callum's eyes widened. Ducking his head out from under Jonah's hand and pulling himself slightly to the side, he said, "You think this is okay? Working for other folks and not getting paid for your labor? Being the property of others?" He gave Jonah a stare of disbelief. How could anyone be so stupid?

Jonah chuckled. "Now, now. It's not as bad as all of that."

"It's worse," Callum countered. "You have a family here. Not me! I don't even know where my family is. I was ripped out of my house while I was sleeping. I don't even know how to get back home if I do run."

"That's just it, Callum! You won't *ever* return to your family. The colonies are your home now. The other slaves and I are the only family members you've got. You might just as well get used to that."

Family members that weren't blood-related and who weren't the same skin color? Callum didn't get it. Nor did he believe Jonah's statement about never seeing his parents and siblings again. They were out there somewhere, and the lad was determined to find them.

Chapter Twenty

A Long Night

The door to Callum's cabin burst open in the middle of the night. This time, it definitely wasn't the wind.

"Guess what day it is, red-leg?" Master Cyrus asked with an obnoxiously wicked laugh.

Rubbing his eyes, Callum said, "I dunno. Saturday?"

"Close. It's Friday, but not just any Friday. It's my birthday. Know what that means, red-leg?"

"No, sir."

"It means you are now my property. My father has given me a couple of acres on the east side of the plantation. You are gonna build a large house for me over there. After that, you're gonna construct a new slave shack for yourself. It'll be half the size of what you have now."

Callum cringed. It had been nearly four months since he had arrived on the plantation. And almost that long since he had first been warned that he had been purchased for Master Cyrus. He threw up in his mouth.

"What are you still in that bed for, red-leg? Get up! We've got work to do."

Furious yet too smart to show it, Callum crawled out from under his blanket and threw his clothes on, "It's still dark out."

Master Cyrus shoved the lad backward, causing him to hit his head against the wall. The planter's son marched over and put a hand just beneath his chin, "The only reason I've been nice to you up to this point is because my father forced me to. But as of today, he has nothing more to say about how I treat you. Don't speak unless you're told to. Not to me, or to anybody else for that matter. Do you hear me?"

Wide-eyed, Callum stood speechless.

Master Cyrus backhanded him, "You failed to answer my question, so I'll ask again. Do you hear me?"

"Yes, sir," Callum said, licking a drop of blood from the corner of his mouth.

"Good. Now, let me make a couple of things clear. I know it's dark. And I'm perfectly aware you haven't had breakfast. You're not gettin' any today. What you're gonna get is a series of lessons in respect and hard labor."

Grabbing Callum's nose and giving it a painful twist, Master Cyrus pulled him out of the cabin. Releasing him, he said, "Today, you'll find out what you're made of."

Callum followed his youthful new owner to the toolshed. "My father's allowin' me to borrow his tools until I get more established. Hold out your arms."

Reluctantly, Callum obeyed. Master Cyrus loaded him up with every piece of equipment they could possibly need. "It'll take us a couple of hours to reach my plot of land. You're carrying the gear. And we're not taking any breaks. You better keep up with me. There's no time to waste."

As Master Cyrus led the way, Callum eyed him from head to toe. Master Cyrus may have been older and taller. He may have known the property better. But he didn't look that tough. And it was doubtful he knew how to defend himself, especially if he were unexpectedly attacked from behind. All he had on him was that horsewhip, and Callum had never seen or even heard of him actually using it on anybody.

Perhaps this was the day Callum had been waiting for. When he would be alone with Master Cyrus, and no one could run to the birthday boy's aid if he were knocked down a peg or two. If the lad were honest with himself, Callum had no desire to kill Master Cyrus; just to turn the tables on him. Well, that, and to acquire his own freedom at the same time.

Whatever Callum was going to do, he couldn't allow the planter's son to suspect a thing. He would have to pretend to fearfully respect Master Cyrus, to obey him as he always had in the past.

Studying Master Cyrus as they journeyed, Callum noted how unobservant he was. Sometimes he would peer off into the distance for ten minutes straight without looking to either side. At others, he went as long as twenty minutes without as much as glancing over his shoulder. Attacking the planter's son wouldn't be that difficult. But if he went that route, how far should he take it? Knock him out? Tie him to a tree? Kill him and hide or maybe burn his body?

Without warning, Master Cyrus stopped in his tracks. Turning to Callum, he asked, "How did Father's shovel get out here?"

Shrugging his shoulders, Callum said, "I don't know."

"I got hit fifteen times with the buckle end of my father's belt for misplacin' his shovel. I've never brought it out here."

Callum turned as white as a ghost. For the second time in one day, he threw up in his mouth. He hated that feeling, though he was certain it didn't feel as bad as being beaten with a belt buckle.

"A while back, you questioned me about those mounds of dirt up ahead," Master Cyrus said. "You've asked other people about 'em as well. Did you sneak out here for a closer look?"

"Na... na... no, sir," Callum stammered. "I would never do that."

Raising both eyebrows, Master Cyrus said, "We'll see about that. Let's go."

To say Callum was scared would be a gross understatement. He didn't know Master Cyrus had taken a whipping on account of his borrowing the shovel. Once the planter's son saw those graves, he'd likely dish out far more lashes than he had received.

Callum's fear turned into courage as he gave the matter more thought. He would not allow Master Cyrus to tear his flesh. It was time to take a stand and in a mighty way.

Master Cyrus interrupted his train of thought as they approached the s, "Drop those tools, and come over here."

"Yes, sir," Callum replied, nervously anticipating the scene about to unfold.

"At first glance, the ground looks untouched. Do you see anything that looks different than when you came by this way a couple of months ago?"

Callum shook his head, "No, sir. Everything appears just as it did."

Master Cyrus inspected mound after mound. "Wait a minute," he said, stopping in front of the one Callum had previously uncovered. "See how this dirt is a shade lighter than the rest?"

Callum knelt down, pretending to examine the soil more closely. Rubbing his hand on the ground, he replied, "No, sir. I don't see any difference."

"You don't, huh?" Master Cyrus chuckled sarcastically. "Really? Grabbing the lad by the nape of the neck, he said, "You heard Father yellin' at me about that shovel. You knew *I* was going to get punished for a crime *you* committed. You let him tan my hide and never spoke up on my behalf. Well, red-leg, I told you earlier that today'll be a day for you to learn a thing or two about respect, and we're gonna start now by giving you a taste of the whip. Fetch the rope so I can secure you to this oak tree right here."

Callum took a deep breath.

Master Cyrus backhanded him again. "Do what I told you, red-leg. Now!"

The courageous side of Callum wanted to beat Cyrus to a bloody pulp. The terrified side of him went for the rope. Picking it up, the lad hesitantly turned to face the planter's son. To his surprise, Master Cyrus was staring at the oak tree, pretending to crack the whip.

That was all the motivation Callum needed! Now he knew what to do. Stealthily, he dropped the rope and exchanged it for a stone before creeping up behind Master Cyrus.

"Hurry up!" Master Cyrus shouted, turning to face him.

As he spun around, Callum smashed the stone against his face, knocking him to the ground.

Dazed, Master Cyrus didn't move a muscle.

It was decision time. Callum had already come up with three options. The easiest, of course, would be to run as fast as he could. The next would be to outright kill his young master, do away with the body, and then return to the main plantation and make up some story about his whereabouts. But the third option seemed like the way to go.

While Master Cyrus remained in a stupor, Callum rolled him onto his belly, dragged him toward the old oak tree, and secured him to it.

Once Master Cyrus came back to, he was going to find himself getting his flesh torn open. Oh, how the tables had been turned!

The lad walked back to the whip and cautiously lifted it off the ground; it was heavier than he thought it would be.

Master Cyrus was beginning to fidget. "Wha... What happened?" he whimpered.

"Oh, it's not what happened," Callum said. "It's what's *about* to."

Master Cyrus was able to turn his head just enough to make eye contact with Callum.

Callum drew the whip back, and just as he was about to strike Master Cyrus for the first time, WHAM! He was on the ground himself. Opening his eyes, he found Master Cyrus standing over him. "I thought you learned your lesson a long time ago, red-leg! You can't be sleepin' all day. There's work to do! Get up!"

For a moment, Callum was disoriented. Then he got it; he was on the floor of his cabin. Everything he had just experienced was a nightmare. Either that or a vision warning him of troubles to come.

Chapter Twenty-One
CHANGE OF PACE

Young ladies didn't come any fairer than Annabel Murphy. Callum found everything about her appealing: her girly giggle, the way she wore that red ribbon in her hair like the girl in the picture, even how she raised one eyebrow and gave him that dirty look every time he tried to get her attention. The only thing Callum didn't like was that she and her brother were only going to be staying with the Gillcrests for a few days. How would he ever get a chance to build a relationship with Annabel in such a short period of time? Especially when he worked the field from the time the sun rose until it set.

Fortunately for Callum, a little scheming could drastically change the order of things. And he didn't feel the slightest bit guilty about getting even with the guy who punished him under false pretenses. He nearly laughed out loud when Master Cyrus released a pain-filled groan, grabbed his stomach, and made a mad dash toward the outhouse.

"Follow him, Callum," Master Josiah ordered. "Make sure he's okay."

"Right away, sir," Callum replied, pretending to care and darting after the planter's son. "What's the matter, Master Cyrus? Everything okay?"

Master Cyrus didn't answer. He did stop, though, just long enough to vomit. His face was breaking out in a sweat.

"Your face is turning green, Master Cyrus. Do you need anything?"

The planter's son grabbed his stomach again and ran closer to the outhouse, with Callum trailing close behind. Master Cyrus stumbled over a stone and humorously attempted to keep himself from falling. His arms flailed every which direction until he eventually landed with a thud.

Callum remembered the dream. As much as he wanted to turn it into a reality, he couldn't do it. Besides, he would never get away with giving Master Cyrus the beating he so richly deserved. He had already paid him back anyway. Slipping those pokeweed berries into Cyrus's stew hadn't been an easy task, but the first part of his plan had come to fruition.

Now to see how good of a faker he could be! Callum ran up next to the planter's son. "Oh, Master Cyrus! I'm so sorry. Do you want me to fetch Mistress Rosanna?"

"No, red-leg. Just help me get into the a... a... out—" Master Cyrus vomited again.

As the sick seventeen-year-old attempted to roll out of the mess, he noticed what Callum hoped he wouldn't. There, in a puddle of vomit, were two intact pokeweed berries.

"What's that?" Master Cyrus asked, pointing at one of them.

"I don't know. A grape, maybe?" Callum asked.

"I didn't eat any grapes, red-leg."

"Maybe your mother mixed them in with something."

"She wouldn't do that. I'm allergic to grapes. I'll tell you what this is — it's pokeweed berries."

Callum feared he might fall into the pit he had dug for Master Cyrus. Talking himself out of this one would take skill. "What's a pokeweed berry? I don't think they had those in Dublin."

Master Cyrus crawled into the outhouse and pulled the door shut behind him without answering. Less than a minute later, the sounds and odor seeping out of the outhouse told Callum those pokeweed berries were working overtime.

Standing outside, the lad heard a loud paaarp, followed by a louder braaap! How disgusting yet funny! Callum giggled but tried to do so quietly. Another braaap and the lad couldn't help but picture the horrible faces Master Cyrus must have been making inside. It served him right!

By the time Master Cyrus made it out of the outhouse, the berries were the last thing on his mind. "I'm weak, red-leg. Come over here, and let me lean on your shoulder. I need help gettin' back to the house."

"Yes, sir," Callum said, feeling more confident the second phase of his plan might work. If the planter's son stayed sick long enough, somebody would have to care for him. And if

Master Cyrus could choose anybody to wait on him hand and foot, Callum was confident he would be the spoiled teen's number one choice.

As the two approached the house, Mistress Rosanna came running. "What happened, Cyrus? What's wrong with you, baby?"

"I don't know," he whined. "I feel horrible."

Mistress Rosanna felt his forehead. "We need to get you into bed."

"That's where I'm headed."

As they continued walking, Callum heard Mistress Rosanna whispering to Master Josiah. She was anything but a quiet whisperer. "You don't think it's yellow fever, do you?"

Callum couldn't hear Master Josiah's response. But Mistress Rosanna was worried, "How about malaria? What are we going to do if whatever he has starts spreading?"

Mistress Rosanna's whispering grew louder as the young men got further away from her, "He's been leaning on Callum. You know what that means? If it's going to spread, we know who will catch it next."

Master Josiah finally spoke at a volume where Callum could make out his words, "That's enough, Rosanna! Every time somebody gets a sniffle, you assume they have something that will kill us all. Every person on this plantation has gotten sick before, and we're still here."

"Really?" Mistress Rosanna shouted. "We're *all* still here?"

"Woman, you need to leave the past where it belongs! What we're talkin' about has nothin' to do with that, and you know it. There's no need to be frettin' over somebody getting sick."

For once, Callum was thankful he was in the room with Master Cyrus instead of the living room with the adults. That was one war he didn't want to be involved in.

"Callum," Mistress Rosanna shouted. "As soon as you get him into bed, you come out here right away."

"Yes, ma'am," Callum called back. "Do you need anything else, Master Cyrus?"

"To be left alone, red-leg. Now, get!" Master Cyrus grumbled.

Callum could only hope the illness would stick around a while, so he could have time to hang around the house pretending to care for the planter's son while making a good impression on a particular young lady.

"How are you feeling, Callum?" Mistress Rosanna asked as soon as he left Master Cyrus's side.

"Good."

Mistress Rosanna felt his forehead, "You don't feel feverish. Do you have any aches or pains?"

"No, ma'am. I'm good."

Just as the words fell from Callum's tongue, in walked Annabel Murphy. Amazingly enough, the sparkle didn't leave her eye even when she was flustered. "Mistress Rosanna, I heard some talk outside that Cyrus might have malaria? Momma wouldn't want me around anything like that. Are you planning to quarantine?"

"Now, now, Annabel," Master Josiah interrupted. "Nobody has malaria, and there's no need for quarantine. Ignore idle tales floating around."

"Idle tales?" Mistress Rosanna scoffed. "Let's be honest. We don't know what Master Cyrus has come down with. It's too early to know whether or not we will quarantine. We're going to send for Doctor Gills."

Master Josiah crossed his arms, "We're doing *what?*"

Annabel giggled, "You two aren't going to fight, are you? Momma warned me about Uncle Josiah's temper."

"She did, did she?" Master Josiah said. "And what else did my charming little sister tell you?"

"Well—" Annabel replied, "On second thought, I probably shouldn't say. I wouldn't want to upset you more than I already have."

Master Josiah's eyes widened. "Oh, I think you had better say, and right now, Annabel! While we're waiting for your parents to return from their trip, you're staying under my roof, and you will answer any questions you're asked. Now, what else did your momma say about me?"

Giggling again, Annabel said, "That a big vein bulges out of your forehead when you get upset. It looks like she was right."

CHAPTER TWENTY-TWO

RUMOR MILL

A twelve-year-old Irish slave driving a carriage off his master's plantation would most likely be looked upon through eyes of suspicion. Callum knew that, as did the Gillcrests. But as far as Mistress Rosanna was concerned, that was their best option. Callum was grateful she took the time to give him a few pointers on how to drive before he took off this time.

He also appreciated the information they gave him about the neighboring plantations – one in particular. "Master Alloway and his wife are the poor, ignorant type. They'll never amount to anything," Master Josiah told him. "I'd be surprised if they have enough smarts to know how to build an outhouse. Not to mention their son. What's his name, Rosanna?"

"Clement," Mrs. Rosanna replied. "Let's not get into all of that. The lad needs to get going."

"I know," Master Josiah said. "He does. But I can't send him past the Alloway's without warning him about that boy of theirs. Listen up, now, Callum. Clement will come across as a nice, helpful type of fellow. But in all reality, he's as low down as a rattlesnake. If at all possible, avoid that boy. For that matter, avoid all of the Alloways. But if you do somehow find yourself in a conversation with Clement, don't trust anything he tells you. He doesn't care about anybody but himself."

"My husband's right," Mrs. Rosanna said. "That Clement is downright dirty. Stay away from him. Now you need to get out of here and fetch the doctor."

"Not so fast," Master Josiah said. "If you try to escape or if this horse gets hurt, you will be brought back here to pay for your crimes, and you will pay with your life." Master Josiah must have been able to read Callum's thoughts because he added, "I'm not referring to a fast death either. Any rebellion and you will be burned, whipped, nearly drowned, and eventually starved to death. What I'm saying,

Callum, is my wife and I are putting a lot of trust in you. Don't disappoint us."

"Yes, sir," Callum said, grabbing the reins and beginning his journey.

As anxious as the lad was to run away, this wasn't the time. It wasn't that the threats scared him out of it. It had more to do with the fact that Ms. Annabel Murphy was visiting. Callum might not have known where his family was, but he knew precisely where that girl would be waiting. He just wished his plan of spending more time with her hadn't backfired.

As long as nobody found out what Callum did with those pokeweed berries, he might be able to impress Annabel with his level of maturity and trustworthiness. Who was he kidding? What colonial girl would be interested in a poor-white earth scratching scum like himself? Callum sighed while coming upon a plantation Master Josiah had told him about. A widow and nearly one hundred smoked Irish slaves lived there. Apparently, the woman felt Irish slaves were too much trouble and not hard enough workers to bother with. If that's how she felt about the Irish, Callum didn't want anything to do with her.

The widow, at least from what Callum could see in passing, had quite the spread. Her plantation house was ten times the size of the Gillcrest's. Tobacco fields stretched out as far as the eye could see, and slaves were hard at work.

The lad continued his journey for another three hours before coming upon a second plantation. He slowed to take a closer look even though Master Josiah had told him Doctor Gills was staying at the third one. A voice suddenly hollered, "Whoa! Whoa there!"

Moving his eyes from plantation to road, Callum saw a man he guessed to be in his upper teens or early twenties standing just in front of his carriage with a hand up. Fearing the young fellow thought he was a runaway, Callum hesitantly pulled back on the reins.

"This looks like Josiah Gillcrest's carriage," the stranger said as the horse came to a halt.

"It is, sir."

"And you must be his new servant?"

"Yes, sir. I really must needs to be on my way. Master Cyrus is sick, and I've been sent for Doctor Gills."

The man smiled. "You're in luck, lad. Doctor Gills is here at my place. Do you mind if I hop up there with you?"

Callum wasn't sure what to think. Master Josiah had told him to keep going until he got to the third plantation. But if the doctor was at the second one and he drove a few hours to the next one, he could find himself in a heap of trouble. "Sure, get in," he said.

As the young man hopped into the carriage, he stuck his hand out. "I'm Clement. What's your name?"

"Callum," the lad answered timidly before swallowing hard. How had he just invited the poor, ignorant, self-centered young man the Gillcrests had warned him to stay away from right into his cart?

"Nice to meet you, Callum. See that carriage way over yonder between those two tall pines?"

Pretending nothing was wrong, Callum said, "Yes, yes, sir."

"That carriage belongs to Doc Gills. Head that direction."

Callum was terrified of the young man. If he was as dangerous as the Gillcrests said he was, that carriage he pointed to might not have had anything to do with the doctor at all. Heading so far into the Alloway property could prove a fatal mistake. What choice did he have? It wasn't like he could push the man out of his cart and take off in another direction! Hesitantly, Callum turned the horses and drove toward the carriage that allegedly belonged to Doc Gills.

"So, how are the Gillcrests treating you?" Clement asked.

No matter how kind that man's voice was, and even though he was the first person in the colonies to take what could be a genuine interest in him, Callum didn't trust the man. "They're treating me fine, sir."

"Glad to hear it.

You seem to be pretty good with Abigail here. How long have you been ridin' horses?"

"Not long," Callum admitted. "Mistress Rosanna taught me so I could make this trip."

Clement chuckled. "You must be a brave lad. Either that or they're looking for a – Maybe I should be asking how many times they've taken the whip to you?"

What a strange, random question! "They haven't, sir," Callum replied.

"They haven't? I don't know the Gillcrests very well. But I've heard things about those folks. You be careful up there. Ya hear me?"

Callum was confused. The Gillcrests said Clement couldn't be trusted, and now Clement was saying the same thing about the Gillcrests. If Darcy were there, she'd have told him that's why a person should never listen to only one side of a story.

Clement didn't seem half as bad as he was made out to be. Perhaps a little conversation would help Callum get a better feel for his personality. And if he asked the right questions and got the right answers, it might just help him unravel a mystery or two.

"Can I ask you a question?" he asked.

"Sounds like you just did, there, lad."

Callum grinned. "So I did. Can I ask you another one?"

"You just did," Clement repeated himself.

Callum couldn't help but chuckle. "What I mean is, I've seen pictures at the Gillcrest's place of other children. But I don't see any around. If Master Cyrus is an only child, who are the kids in all those pictures?"

Clement scratched his chin and peered off into the distance.

"I'm sorry," Callum said. "I shouldn't have asked."

"No, it's okay," Clement replied. "I was trying to decide whether or not you're old enough to hear a story like that. How old are you, lad?"

Callum hadn't given his age much thought for quite some time. "Twelve or thirteen."

"You don't know which?"

"No, sir. I don't know what month it is."

"Today is September 7th. How old does that make you?"

Callum smiled. "That means I'm still twelve. I won't be thirteen until October 2nd."

"You're getting old, lad."

Callum caught on to what he was doing. Clement was trying to change the subject. He decided to use the man's own words against him.

"You're right; I am getting old. And if I'm old, that means I can hear about those kids at the Gillcrest's place."

Clement laughed. "We're getting close to Doc Gill. Promise not to say a word to anybody if I tell you what I know?"

"Promise," Callum agreed.

"Alright, lad. Here it is. The Gillcrests used to have six or seven children running around their plantation. One by one, they've disappeared. The first one supposedly ran away from home. They said he told his siblings he was tired of getting whipped for every little thing he did. Then there was that girl. Oh, I can't remember any of their names right now. But she was close to your age the last time my family saw her. Rumor has it she wandered off in the woods alone, and nobody ever caught sight of her again. There was a toddler. Allegedly, she fell into the well. Josiah said they were able to get her body out somehow, and they gave her a private burial somewhere. Listen, there's Doc Gill. We can't let him know we're talking about this stuff. This conversation stays between the two of us."

"Yes, sir," Callum said.

"Doc Gill!" Clement shouted. "Looks like there might be an emergency out at the Gillcrest plantation!"

Chapter Twenty-Three

QUARANTINE

While Doc Gill and the adult Gillcrests were in the room tending to Master Cyrus, Callum finally got his chance. "Cute dress," he said.

Annabel blushed.

"It looks perfect on you," Callum added.

Annabel's cheeks turned a deeper shade of pink. "Thank you."

Callum was proud of himself. He had gotten up his nerve to tell her how he felt. Well, kind of anyway. If only the lad could find a way to start a conversation with her. That would be the key to creating a relationship. It was worth a shot. "If you're still around Sunday, I'd like to take you for a walk. I have something to show you."

"Really? What is it?"

"Something I found a couple of months ago. I've talked to people about it but haven't shown anybody."

"Are you gonna tell me what it is or just keep me guessing?" Annabel asked.

"I'm not exactly sure. But I suspect it's a bunch of graves."

Oops. The expression on Annabel's face told Callum he had made a mistake. Perhaps girls weren't too keen on checking out burial grounds. Who would have known?

Levi, Annabel's brother, stepped between them. "Is that supposed to be funny?"

"No. I thought they were interesting and that she'd think so too."

Levi looked Callum over from head to toe. "If that's the case, why didn't you offer to show them to me?"

Callum shrugged. "I don't know." Sporting an ornery smile, he said, "Maybe because *you* don't look like *her*."

Levi and Annabel glanced at each other for a second, and both burst into laughter. Laughter that told Callum he had come across as immature. As not being a lady's man. As being no more than they had initially thought — an ignorant red-leg.

Master Josiah entered the hallway. "Callum, thank you for fetching the doctor. Your service is no longer needed. Get out to the field. Jonah will tell you what to do."

"Yes, sir."

"As for you two," Master Josiah continued, "Cyrus is very ill. This is not a time for laughter. There are potatoes in the kitchen that need peeling. Since your hands are idle, get to it."

Now Annabel would never give Callum a chance! Not only had he invited her to see graves, but he had gotten her and Levi in trouble with her uncle. Maybe there was a way he could make it up to her.

Callum left the house as Annabel and Levi marched toward the kitchen. With the sun already setting, Callum knew there wasn't much work-time left. Wasting no time, he headed toward the other workers, wondering what he could do to patch things up with the planter's niece. Levi seemed like he could be interested in seeing the mounds of dirt. Maybe if he took Levi to see them, Annabel would come along, and he could win her over with conversation on the way to and from? The only problem with that plan was that Callum wasn't sure all the dirt mounds contained bodies. What if they got out there and Levi insisted on digging into a few of them, and it turned out to be nothing? That wasn't a risk the lad was willing to take. There had to be another way.

As Callum got closer to the field, all the slaves stopped working. "Master Cyrus is okay," Callum said. "The doctor says he'll be back on his feet in no time."

No smiles, no cheers, no words. Everybody returned to work as if it were any other ordinary day. "Jonah, Master Cyrus said you would tell me what to do. I'm ready to work."

"It's about time, lad. There's only an hour of daylight left. Gather up the tools and get them back to the shed."

Even though it was somewhat typical for Jonah to be so straightforward, he sounded more agitated than Callum had seen him in a while. "Right away, sir," the lad said.

As Callum collected tools, he learned Jonah wasn't the only one who was sore with him. It seemed like everywhere he turned, someone was scolding him or at least mumbling something beneath their breath. "Why on earth he sent the new lad is beyond me!" one said. "Letting him skip out on an entire day of work." Another gave him an evil glare, saying, "We haven't been able to eat anything since you left.

Master Josiah was afraid you'd run off, and he's taken it out on the rest of us all day!"

First it was Annabel, and now everyone else. Trying to appease the others as best as possible, the lad rushed to collect their tools at lightning speed.

Carrying everything he could, he made his way toward the tools shed, feeling as though the weight of the world was on his shoulders. How was it that wherever he was, he could become the people's number one enemy? Callum felt like he could cry at any given moment. Life was so unfair. The sad part was, it had been that way since the day he was born. Not that having a pity party would make things any better.

As Callum passed the plantation house, Master Josiah met him outside. "Doc thinks Cyrus has a mild case of influenza."

Influenza? What kind of word was that? "Is influenza serious?" Callum asked.

"Could be."

Not wanting anybody else to be upset with him, the lad fell back into his acting routine, "Is there anything I can do?"

"Doc says we need to quarantine Cyrus, and if anybody else shows signs of illness, they'll have to join him. For the time being, you're going to move in with Jonah and his family. Your cabin will become the quarantine shelter."

"But Master Cyrus just —"

"He just *what*, Callum?"

"I... um... Doctor Gill just got here. How does he already know it's influenza?"

"He's seen it before, I suppose," Master Josiah said. "Let me break the news to Jonah myself. Go ahead and get those tools put away."

What rotten timing! On the very night Jonah and the rest of the slaves were upset with him, they would have to start sharing the same living quarters? Things could have been worse. The lad could have had to go into quarantine himself for being so close to the planter's son. Worse, Master Cyrus could have remembered seeing those berries, and then Callum would have had serious explaining to do.

Now things could have been better too. Master Josiah could have told Callum to sleep in the main house, where he could have had a chance to patch things up with Annabel. But that was okay. The damage had already been done, and it was unlikely the lad could fix the situation with the short time left before her departure.

Callum continued his trip to the toolshed. He didn't understand why everyone was so mad anyway. It wasn't like he had asked to drive the carriage or that driving that thing all day wasn't a job of its own. That would be like Callum getting upset because they didn't drive the carriage like he had to do.

Putting the tools away, the lad convinced himself that staying with Jonah could even turn into a good thing. That man had the answers he was looking for. If only the lad could find a way to get him to open up!

Closing the toolshed, Callum decided to kill time by looking for another turtle. With Master Cyrus off his feet and Master Josiah explicitly saying he needed a few minutes to speak with Jonah, the timing couldn't have been more perfect. And besides, even girls liked turtles! Maybe that was a way to reach Annabel's heart.

With his eyes as wide as saucers, the lad tried to cover as much ground as possible before it got dark. He checked open grassy areas, inside hollow logs, along the creek bank, and in the forest. If any turtles were around, they were deliberately staying out of his sight. Word had probably gotten out about what happened to the last one he found!

Once Callum was sure Master Josiah had plenty of time to break the news to Jonah, he headed toward his new temporary quarters.

Jonah was waiting just outside the door. "Welcome to *our* house," he said. "You are not here by our choice, but because Master Josiah said we *must* allow you to stay. You are *not* a part of our family, yet you *will* abide by our every rule and expectation."

So good to the thought staying with Jonah might turn into a good thing! Seeking peace, the lad lowered his eyes and said, "Yes, sir. I understand."

In a gruff, uncaring voice, Jonah added, "We don't have any extra beds, and my daughter isn't giving hers up for a white nigger like yourself. Sleep on the floor." Jonah turned and opened the door while grumbling, "Why couldn't Master Josiah put you in Ghazi's cabin. He has one all to himself!"

The beginning of Callum's stay in his new temporary cabin may not have gotten off to a smooth start, but it was only the first night. The lad was confident Jonah would warm up to him as time passed.

CHAPTER TWENTY-FOUR

BUSTED

It may have taken four days to get there, but young Callum McCarthy was finally to the place where he could speak somewhat freely with Jonah. "Accepting my life as a slave is something I'm not willing to do. With or without your help, I *will* find a way off this plantation."

Jonah closed his eyes and took a deep breath before responding in exasperation, "You are one of the most stubborn white niggers I've ever met! Let me show you somethin', lad." Turning his back, Jonah took his shirt off.

Callum couldn't believe it. A crisscross pattern of vicious scars decorated the man's back. "How many times did you try to escape?"

Jonah turned back around to face Callum. "None. Six years ago, Master Josiah's son vanished without a trace. Master Cyrus said he ran away and claimed I knew all about it. Master Josiah asked me what I knew, and I told him — absolutely nothing."

Callum was outraged. Never had he seen or heard a tale of anything so detestable. "Master Josiah did this to you? Because you didn't know anything?"

Jonah shook his head, "Because he thought I was withholding information. My back will never be the same. Are you prepared to have your flesh look like mine for the rest of your days?"

Callum's eyes welled up with tears. Here he had thought Master Josiah was a semi-decent man. How could he do something so terrible to another human being? Especially with no proof of wrongdoing? As far as Jonah's question was concerned, having his back look like that wouldn't be pleasant, but it wasn't like he could ever see his own back anyway. More worrisome was how it might feel.

"Do you seriously have to think about the answer? Let me help you. No, Callum. You're *not* ready for that. You have your whole life ahead of you; the fewer scars you get, the better. You're a slave now; you'll still be a slave tomorrow and every day for the rest of your life. Get used to it."

"No," Callum protested. "I'm a slave today and I will be a slave tomorrow. But I will *not* be a slave forever. I *will* escape, and I *will* be a free man. I might even switch places with the Gillcrests. You understand me, right? There's more of us than there are of them! We could do it tonight if you were willing to. We could overtake the Gillcrests. We would own this whole plantation, and *they* would work for *us*!"

Jonah's face filled with disgust. "Callum, you've never had a whip taken to you. You have no idea how it's going to feel the first time you get caught trying anything so foolish or even get caught talking about it. Speaking of which, we need to stop this conversation now. Master Josiah's coming our way. Get to harvesting!"

Callum pulled off more tobacco leaves. He had indeed been talking far too long, and it showed. If he didn't add a lot more leaves to his pile before Master Josiah got over there, he was going to be in trouble.

Then again, it was possible he would be in trouble before Master Josiah got to him. "Callum!" the planter called. "Stop what you're doing and get over here!"

That man sounded angry. Beyond angry.

"Good news and bad news," Jonah said gruffly. "Good news is, he doesn't have a whip with him. Bad news, he's got a doubled-over belt in his hand. My guess is you're about to get a good hiding, and due to your age and inexperience on the plantation, he's going to show you mercy. Whatever it's for, don't resist – no matter how bad it hurts. Learn from it."

"Callum!" Master Josiah shouted, louder and more furiously than before. "Hustle! Move those feet *NOW!*"

Without wasting another second, Callum dropped his sack and sprinted toward Master Josiah. There had been a few times since arriving at the Gillcrest plantation that the lad thought he was going to get it and get it good. So far, he had been fortunate enough to get off with warnings, except for those times when Master Cyrus had backhanded or shoved him anyway. In all of the other close-calls, Callum had understood why someone was upset with him. Not this time.

The lad's eyes weren't as good as Jonah's. For the first time, after running for several minutes, he was just beginning to see that belt Jonah had referred to. Seeing it slowed his pace — not out of defiance but fear. He thought back to the sketches, the graves, the warning Clement had given him, and those scars on Jonah's back.

"I didn't say you could slow down! Hurry it up, red-leg!"

Regardless of his onsetting nausea, Callum knew he had to comply. He didn't slow down or stop until standing directly in front of Master Josiah. To his shock, the planter didn't ask him a question or even give him a lecture. Instead, he grabbed Callum's arm, spun him around, and began viciously lashing his backside with that belt. After ten lashes, he stopped swinging but kept Callum in position for more. "I've been made aware of some misbehavior on your part, Callum. You better start confessing. What have you done?"

Couldn't Master Cyrus have asked him about something specific? That would have made Callum feel much better. The belt connected again and stung far worse than the others had. "Answer me, Callum!" He brought the belt down again. "Tell me how you've been misbehaving!"

Callum didn't want to cry, but he did. Not only because of the pain but because he didn't know how long this might go on. "I... uncovered... one of the mounds of dirt on your property, sir."

Master Josiah gave him another beating. "And you allowed Cyrus to get in trouble for losing my shovel, didn't you?"

Now sobbing, Callum struggled to speak, "I... da... did... I... I... I'm sor... sorry."

Master Josiah gripped the lad's arm tighter and brought the belt back in preparation for another swing. Callum jerked his hips forward even though the belt didn't move. Master Josiah held it there, awaiting Callum's response.

"I..." Callum's voice trembled. "I... put pokeweed berries in your son's stew."

"Yes, you did, Callum!" he said, striking him several more times. "And why would you do such a foolish thing?"

Terrified to tell the truth and terrified to lie, Callum stood silently for a moment. Master Josiah gave him three more lashes. Callum didn't know how it was possible, but it seemed Master Josiah used more strength the longer the whipping continued. "Out with it!" he shouted.

"Oooh... Oooh... I..." Callum sniffled. "I... wanted a reason... to stay closer to the plantation house... so I could... be around Annabel."

Master Josiah struck him five more times before dropping the belt and spinning Callum back around to face him. Using the hand that had previously held the belt, he grabbed the lad's other arm and shook him violently for a second, "You could have murdered my son. Do you understand me?"

"I was just trying to make him sick, not kill him," Callum whined.

"Fortunately for you, he's recovering! Doctor Gill says he should be back on his feet within the next few days. If he had died, I would have slain you with my bare hands. Don't you doubt that for a moment! I can be the nicest man you'll ever meet, or I can be the cruelest. Your behavior will decide which side of me you will know."

CHAPTER TWENTY-FIVE

MASTER OLIVER

As soon as Callum's eyes popped open, he scanned the room. Thankfully, Jonah was already on his feet and dressed. Callum jumped up and went straight to him, "Good morning, sir."

"Good morning, Callum."

"I couldn't sleep last night. All I kept thinking about was that lad you said ran away. What was he like?"

"Master Oliver?" Jonah chuckled. "He was quite the lad! I'll tell you this much. He wasn't anything like the rest of them Gillcrests."

"What do you mean?" Callum asked.

"He was kind and gentle, finding something to laugh about pretty much every day. He was one of those boys that always had his pockets full. He didn't care if it was a toad, a glob of mud, a feather, his sling, or that ball he was always playing with. Something was always in those pockets of his."

"So, Master Oliver was a happy kid?"

"For the most part, he was," Jonah said.

Callum scratched his head, "If he was so happy, why would he run away?"

"I didn't say he did," Jonah replied. "I said Master Oliver vanished, and Master Cyrus *claimed* he ran away."

Callum slipped his shirt on. "So, you don't think he ran off? What do you think happened to him then?"

"I don't like to speculate," Jonah said. "All I can tell you is he's not here anymore."

Callum couldn't let it go, and since Jonah didn't seem to mind the questioning, he continued his inquiry. "You said Master Oliver wasn't like the other Gillcrests? Did he get along with them?"

Jonah shook his head as he attached his suspenders, "Not really," he said. "That lad got more whippings than all the other children combined, most of 'em undeserved."

Callum had no trouble relating to that one. Maybe he and Master Oliver were more alike than he realized. Perhaps that's why Master Cyrus was always looking for a reason to whip him. Because he reminded him so much of his brother. "They whipped him for no reason?"

"Oh, they had their reasons, alright! He was talking too much. Getting too distracted to complete his work assignments. Spilling things. Most of the time, it seemed he got in trouble just for being a lad. But then there were the other occasions. One time, for example, it was because he was out there playing with that ball of his. I'll tell you what, that ball got Master Oliver in trouble more than anything else. Anyway, he was tossing it up in the air and catching it over and over again. That thing came down at precisely the wrong time and cracked Mistress Rosanna upside the head. Oh, man! Let me tell you. Master Josiah was furious. For whatever reason, he didn't have his belt on that day, but he took Master Oliver across his knee and whipped that boy's behind so hard

I doubt he even tried to sit down for the next three days."

Regardless of how Jonah saw it, Callum could understand why Master Josiah had whipped him over that one. A ball cracking his wife in the head? It could have killed her! "Did he come up missing after that?" Callum asked.

"Listen, lad, we can't keep this conversation going all day. Most everybody else is already over at the plantation house. So, I'll tell ya this one more story, and then we've got to get moving. Okay?"

"Yes, sir," Callum said.

"Now mind you, what I'm about to tell you, we're not supposed to talk about. So don't you go flapping those gums to nobody, or we're both going to be attached to that whipping post."

"I won't tell a soul," Callum promised.

"Good. Remember that quarrel the Gillcrests were having the other day? Well, they were having a feud, kind of like that one. But they were outside and I think Master Josiah might have even been drinking a little. Master Josiah got up in Mistress Rosanna's face, and buddy, I'll tell you one thing. Ole Master Oliver didn't like that very much. He took that sling out of his pocket, put a small stone in it, slang that thing around, and pegged the back of Master Josiah's neck. Master Josiah left yelling at Mistress Rosanna, grabbed hold of Master Oliver's ear, and dragged him into the plantation house. We heard some yelling and screaming. That was the last time any of us slaves saw him."

"But Master Cyrus said he ran away?"

"He did indeed," Jonah said.

CHAPTER TWENTY-SIX

DREAM-LEGS

Birthdays come, and birthdays go, but Callum expected his thirteenth to be special. It should have signified a transitional period between being a lad and a man. Somehow, having one with no mother, father, brother, or sister around didn't much feel like a birthday at all.

Of everyone on the plantation, only one seemed to care. "Red-leg, I'm happy for you!" Master Cyrus said. "You know why? Your birthday signifies somethin' significant. Want to know what it is?"

"What's that?" Callum asked.

"In two short months, you'll belong to me. And you better believe I've been keeping a journal about all the beatings you deserve once it's up to me how, when, and where you receive them. *Happy birthday, red-leg!*"

The planter's son sure was holding to that story. Callum was starting to think he was telling the truth. If he was, two months wasn't much time, especially with Master Cyrus's personal vendetta against him.

The lad's work assignment for the third day in a row was to mend fencing along the eastern border of the Gillcrest plantation. That kind of work not only added more callouses to Callum's hands but gave him more splinters than anything else he had done in his life. As Callum dug his tenth post hole for the morning, a horse trotted up behind him. Turning, the lad was surprised to see a familiar face.

"Callum, right?" Clement asked.

"Yes, sir."

"Are things still going well?"

Callum looked around to make sure he was still alone. Dropping the post he was about to put in, he said, "Not really."

Clement dismounted his horse, "Tell me about it."

Taking a deep breath and hoping he wasn't going to get in trouble for sharing his thoughts,

Callum said, "In two months, Master Cyrus is going to be eighteen."

"And?"

"On the day he turns eighteen, I'm supposed to become his first official slave."

Clement scratched his chin. "How would that be different than serving Master Josiah?"

Looking around once more, Callum replied, "The only thing Master Cyrus likes about me is that I'm smaller than he is. He's already making plans for torturin' me when I become his personal property. I'm afraid he'll murder me if he gets the chance. Oh, and another thing! Those rumors you shared with me might be true. A month or two ago, Master Josiah told me he wouldn't hesitate to kill me with his bare hands if I ever cross him."

Clement ran his fingers through his hair. "I wasn't going to tell you this, lad, but I have to. As before, I need you to keep this between the two of us. Can you handle that?"

"Yes, sir," Callum said.

"Let's have a seat, shall we?"

"I don't know. If Master Josiah or Master Cyrus see me sitting or even talking to you, I could get in big trouble."

"It's okay," Clement said. "We'll both keep an eye out. The second we see somebody, you jump up and start working, and I'll hop right in there and help. I'll say I was driving by, thought I'd lend you a helping hand, and wouldn't take no for an answer."

Callum sure hoped Clement was a man of his word. He could use a break. Cautiously, he sat on an old tree stump while Clement sat on a medium-sized boulder across from him.

"When I was just about your age," Clement said, "my parents sent me to the Gillcrest's place to fetch Mistress Rosanna as my mother was feeling ill, and the doc was nowhere near town. As soon as I arrived at the plantation, an uneasy feeling crept over me. I don't know what Master Josiah was up to, but he must have heard me coming. He came rushin' out from behind his toolshed with a huge vein popping up on his forehead and his eyes all narrow and fierce. As he got closer to me, I couldn't help but notice fresh blood on his shirt. Master Josiah was more nervous than I'd ever seen anybody."

Just hearing the story made Callum nervous. Not just because of this story. Because he had heard, seen, and experienced too many things to doubt the validity of what he was hearing. "Did you ask Master Josiah what was going on?"

"No. I was too afraid to say a word more than I had to. But he asked me questions. Too many for comfort. Master Josiah asked how long I had been there and if I had been snooping around his property. He asked if I'd heard anything unusual as I was drivin' up in my parents' carriage. Every time I answered him, Master Josiah would stare deep into my eyes and say, 'You're not lying to me, now, are you, lad?' Before he went inside to get Mistress Rosanna, he said something I took as a threat, 'Don't you dare tell a soul about the questions I've been askin' or about anything else on this property.' I was so terrified of Master Josiah that I didn't know if I'd make it back home alive. I've been uncomfortable around the man ever since."

Callum wiped the sweat from his brow, "Did you talk to your folks about it?"

"Tried to," Clement said, holding his arm up to block the sun out of his eyes. "But they wouldn't have anything to do with it. My father took a switch to me for backbiting and told me I had better not breathe another word of it to anybody, or he'd give me a second thrashing."

Callum swallowed hard. He didn't know what to say. It sounded as though Clement's family were so busy trying to avoid trouble with the Gillcrests that they would turn their backs on anything that came across as even remotely suspicious.

Not knowing what else to do, Callum stood, picked the post back up, and headed toward the hole he'd dug for it.

"Let me help you with that," Clement said, grabbing the other end. "Have you considered running away before something bad happens to you?"

"I think about it every day, Callum replied. "But I don't have a place to go. I'm afraid of running out of food. And of having no place to sleep when it gets cold out. Could I stay on your plantation?"

Clement chuckled. "Maybe you didn't notice, but my family doesn't have any servants. If somebody saw you there, they'd have no doubt we were harboring a runaway."

"Your family? You don't look old enough to have children."

"I'm eighteen. It's my parents' plantation; I still live with them," Clement said. "I'll promise you this, though. If you ever have an urgent need for a safe retreat, I can hide you out somewhere on our property for a day or two until you can figure out another plan. Unfortunately, that's the best I can offer."

Callum grinned, "Thank you, sir. I'll keep that in mind."

"If you come, do so with the utmost caution. Don't let my folks catch sight of you. They wouldn't see things the way I do and might not be too welcoming."

"Yes, sir. I understand."

"I've kept you from your work long enough now. Besides, I've got some things to tend to myself today. But our paths will cross again soon. In the meantime, keep your eyes open. Be careful out here."

Callum watched as Clement mounted his horse and galloped away. It wasn't a coincidence that the older teenager stopped by when he did. Callum was confident he would eventually use the Alloway's place as a hide-out while heading as far from the Gillcrest plantation as he could get. When, he didn't know. But he was sure it would be sometime before the arrival of Master Cyrus's eighteenth birthday.

Dreams only come true if you put legs on them. That's what Darcy always said anyway. Callum had been thinking of running away or launching an attack on the Gillcrests for months. So far, the dreams had remained legless.

Holding the newly installed post upright, Callum kicked dirt in around it. While steadying the post, he thought it an excellent time to design the legs for his dream.

Thankfully, the lad had earned an enormous amount of trust. Otherwise, Master Josiah wouldn't have chosen him to take the carriage to find Doctor Gill. Nor would he be working so far away from the others without supervision. Other than Jonah, nobody on the plantation would have any reason to suspect he was thinking of fleeing. That would work to his advantage. Being light-skinned like the neighbors was another thing he had going for him, as he could blend in better than a smoked Irish slave could have.

Cold weather would be setting in soon. With limited resources, surviving alone would be difficult. Clement said he could only hide him out for a couple of days. That might be an excellent stopping-off point, but he wouldn't be able to stay there long. Callum needed a better plan. Maybe he could find out where Annabel Murphy lived. Perhaps her family would take him in. If not, he could at least take shelter close by and make it a point to cross paths with her regularly.

That would never work! Annabel and Levi knew he was enslaved. If they saw him, they would tell their parents, who would likely notify a slave catcher or the Gillcrests of his whereabouts.

Callum would have to escape without a final destination in mind. When the timing was right, he would take off on foot, run through a creek, hide out in the woods for a few days, stop by Clement's place to see if he had any suggestions on where to head next, and go from there.

Dream-legs were beginning to sprout!

CHAPTER TWENTY-SEVEN

INCHING
CLOSER

While other slaves busied themselves singing, shouting, and sharing scriptures from the Good Book they didn't really have, Callum sneaked into the toolshed and helped himself to an old hatchet nobody had used the entire time he had been on the plantation. After the whole shovel experience, Callum knew the risks. But he also needed a way to survive on his own.

Slipping the handle in the waistband of his breeches and covering its head with his shirt,

Callum dashed back to his cabin. Inside, with his heart pounding, the lad took it out and slid it under his mattress. Nobody ever looked there.

Callum took a seat on the edge of his bed. If Master Josiah noticed the missing hatchet, Callum would be the primary suspect. One of the Gillcrests would search his cabin with or without his knowledge. He couldn't leave it there. There had to be a better place not only to stash the hatchet but anything else he might need before taking off.

The fence Callum had been mending all week! Yes! That was the answer! The fence ran right alongside the road to the Alloway's plantation. If the lad were to find a place to stockpile his goods in that vicinity, nobody would ever spot them.

Making repeated trips to the fence-line would not only be chancy but downright exhausting. The lad would have to make his first trip worthwhile. While the other slaves continued enjoying their Sunday service, Callum chose his first target — Jonah's cabin. Staying there for ten days had allowed him to scope out the place.

Stealing from Jonah didn't necessarily feel good, but had the man agreed to help Callum escape, it wouldn't have been necessary in the first place. Jonah nor his family would notice if he took that small cob-web-covered tankard out of their cupboard. Swiping it, Callum stuffed the tankard in a breeches pocket while trying to remember what else he had seen that might come in handy.

The lad's mind was drawing a blank. That is until he found a stash of candles. Callum snatched a skinny one and dropped it inside the tankard he had just taken.

A pair of stockings would come in handy! Callum stuffed them in another pocket.

The more he took, the more nervous he became. If someone were to catch him, he would get a severe beating and lose all hope of regaining freedom anytime soon.

Callum crept to the door and peeked around to ensure no one was in sight. Not seeing a soul, he darted back to his cabin and shoved everything he had taken under his bed.

The lad wanted one more thing, but getting it would be highly daring. And it's not like Master Cyrus's pocket watch would help him survive better. It was more of a way to get back at him. Maybe that one could wait.

Callum went outside and sat on the ground next to his cabin. Waiting for nightfall would be the safest way to get his newly claimed belongings to the fence-line. In the meantime, what he needed was rest.

When the slaves concluded their church service, Callum tensely watched Jonah and his family reenter their cabin. How he hoped they wouldn't notice anything missing! Surely, he didn't leave any evidence he'd sneaked into their place.

After three or four minutes of stillness, a hand landed on the lad's shoulder. Callum gasped while turning to face whoever had touched him. It was Ghazi, the other white slave. "Mind if I join you?"

Surprised, Callum said, "You can sit here." The timing was suspicious as he and Ghazi had never had as much as a conversation before.

The other white slave sat on the ground a few inches from Callum, but instead of speaking, stared at the ground blankly.

Callum didn't say anything either. He didn't want to take any chances on spilling information he would later regret. Instead, he gazed off into the distance, hoping Ghazi wouldn't confront him over his thievery.

After several minutes of awkward silence, Ghazi finally spoke, "So, Callum. I'm curious. Why don't you attend church with us?"

Callum chuckled, "I'm not a believer."

"You don't believe God exists?"

"I don't know what I believe," the lad replied. "It just seems a bit far-fetched. To be honest, I'd rather not talk about it."

"As you wish," Ghazi said. "What would you rather talk about?"

Still suspicious of whether Ghazi had somehow seen him in action, Callum chose to take advantage of his question and change the subject, "I'd like to hear your story."

"My story?" Ghazi asked. "About what?"

"About how you got here. You're Irish too, right?"

Ghazi smiled, "I am. The red hair gives me away every time! I got here the same way most Irish did. I was hard up for money, couldn't find a job, and had no way of paying my rent. I kept hearing talk of a land where food and opportunities were aplenty, and I started talking to folks. I found out there were people called spirits who would help me get to the colonies if I agreed to work off the cost of my transportation, but my only pay would be food and a roof over my head."

"So, you agreed to come?"

"I talked to my mother and father first. Neither of them thought it was a good idea. I talked to my siblings and my friends.

Everybody I knew told me anyone with an ounce of common sense would know better than to make such an agreement with a total stranger. But I was tired of being poor. I didn't want to live that way for the rest of my life. So, I signed an agreement to become an indentured servant."

Callum struggled to understand why anyone would volunteer to become enslaved. Ghazi's friends were right. That was a foolish thing to do. How foolish, he wasn't sure. "So, how long have you been at the Gillcrest plantation?"

"Three years down and a little more than seven to go."

"You agreed to be a slave for *ten years* just to get passage into the colonies?"

Ghazi looked at the ground. "No. I agreed to come for five. But I didn't know what I was getting myself into. I'm sure by now you've heard what happened to Jonah's son, right?"

"No, sir," Callum said. "What happened?"

"You're going to find out sooner or later, so you might as well hear it from me. None of us knows for sure what happened, but late one night Master Josiah knocked on Jonah's door. Said Master Cyrus heard some coyotes yippin' the way they always do after a kill. He grabbed the shotgun and ran to the barn to check on the animals. When he got there, he found a bloody mess, and right next to it was an old rabbit's foot John always carried around with him. Jonah checked his cabin, and sure enough, John was missing. Nobody ever saw him again. To be honest, I think that's why Jonah's always sneaking around lookin' after you."

"That's why Jonah does what?"

"You haven't seen him doing his best to keep an eye on you? Why do you think he was so upset when you got back late after going to fetch the doctor? That man was worried sick about you all day. I could see it all over his face."

Callum was confused. "I thought he was mad because I didn't work the field when everybody else did."

"Really? I'm a light sleeper. There have been nights when I've seen people sneaking around. Master Cyrus and you in particular. But you know what I've noticed? Whenever you sneak off somewhere, if Jonah catches wind of it, he sneaks off behind you. I think that man has assigned himself the responsibility of making sure nothing tragic happens to you."

That got Callum thinking. His door whipping open in the middle of the night, and nobody being there. Seeing something dart behind a tree out in the woods. Getting dragged out of the river and placed back on that burial mound. Could Jonah have been behind all of that? "Can I ask your opinion on something?" he asked.

"What's that, lad?"

"If I tell you about something, you have to keep your mouth closed."

"I've already been doing that, Callum. What is it?"

"One night, I was out in the woods doing something I shouldn't have been that I don't feel like talking about. On my way home, I fell into a stream and must've hit my head on something and passed out. When I woke up, I was right back at the scene of the bad thing I did. Somebody had to have pulled me out of the water and taken me there. Can you think of any reason why Jonah would have done such a thing?"

Ghazi glanced toward Jonah's shack for a moment before looking back at Callum. "Probably because he knows you're every bit as stubborn as John was."

"What's that supposed to mean?"

"Had Jonah told John not to do something, John would have sneaked off and done it anyhow. Ole Jonah probably figured instead of telling you to stay home at night, he'd put a little fear in you. Creep you out a little bit to teach you a lesson. But that hasn't worked either, has it?"

Callum chuckled and shook his head, "I guess not." He couldn't believe how stupid he had been. How had he not realized how hard Jonah had been working to keep the lad above ground? Jonah, the man he had just stolen from, had been acting as a substitute father figure, and it had slipped right over his head.

Too embarrassed to say so, Callum said, "I didn't mean to get you completely off topic. I think you were trying to tell me something else about John?"

"That's okay, Callum," Ghazi said. "I pretty much told you what I was going to about him. The only other thing I was going to say is that I was never convinced John really died because of coyotes. Being the light sleeper I am, if coyotes were yipping, I'd have heard them. And everything was quiet that night. Not knowing what really happened to that lad, I changed my mind about being an indentured servant and begged to go home. Master Josiah insisted that was out of the question. He had paid a price for me; to get his money's worth, he was supposed to get five years of labor out of me. For the next couple of months, I was miserable. I hated

Master Josiah, his family, and even the other slaves. I decided to break away from this place."

That got Callum's attention. "Did you do it?"

"I tried to. One morning, when I thought nobody was looking, I took off. I hadn't gotten far when somebody hollered, 'Ghazi's running!' Looking over my shoulder, I felt like an enormous army was coming after me. The next thing I remember is waking up tied to a whipping post."

That wasn't exactly what Callum wanted to hear. "How bad did they whip you?"

"Put it this way. That hiding Master Josiah gave you with his belt a while back was like having somebody tap the top of your hand in comparison to what I went through. Blood poured all over my body. I was screaming and begging for his mercy. That man beat on me so long I didn't think I'd live through it. And I'm not exaggerating."

Callum swallowed hard. "I'm sorry, Ghazi."

"That's not the worst of it. I never learned how to read or write. When I signed that agreement to become an indentured servant, the spirit never explained that the Gillcrests could extend my time of servitude if I ran. And that's what he did. Master Josiah is forcing me to serve him longer because of the act of what he called rebellion. Had I not run, I'd only have two more years of this. But now I have seven, and there's nobody to blame but myself."

"They tricked you," Callum said. "That's not your fault. I'd be ready to kill somebody."

"Things could be worse."

Callum shook his head.

"Have you not seen that letter R on Caspar's face? When he tried to escape, Master Josiah branded him as a runaway in case he ever took off again. I'm thankful my face hasn't been scarred up like that."

Callum ran his fingers through his hair. "You both ran away but didn't receive the same punishment?"

"Supposedly, Caspar ran away twice before getting his R. Since I only ran once, I was spared that part of the punishment."

Chapter Twenty-Eight

GOING FOR IT

Being beaten to a bloody pulp and having his time extended for seeking freedom was too brutal for words. Still, it gave Callum more to think about. That hiding he had gotten for the shovel and the pokeweed berries had taken the lad well beyond the threshold he had for pain. He couldn't even imagine what it would feel like to be beaten the way both Ghazi and Jonah had been. Then again, both had been lashed by the same master Callum was now serving. If he continued residing there, a day would come when he too could illustrate a story with everlasting scars of torment.

There are times in life, however, when a person cannot permit the fears of what *could* happen to get in the way of progress. This was one of those moments. Yes, if Callum got caught running away, he could bring more pain upon himself than he could bear. On the other hand, staying on the plantation would guarantee a lifetime of harsh bondage. One way there was hope for freedom. The other way, hope was nonexistent.

Today Callum would find out what he was or wasn't made of. Tightly gripping the ax handle, he yanked the blade out of the round of fir he had attempted to split. Per Master Cyrus's orders, all one-hundred-and-fifty rounds had to be split and neatly stacked behind the plantation house by nightfall.

"You're never gonna finish in time if you don't put more muscle into it than that," Master Cyrus scoffed. "I've seen 85-year-old women split wood faster than you do."

The plan only called for running away, but it wasn't too late to add to that plan. Wood wasn't the only thing that ax would be able to split wide open. Callum forced himself to remain stone-faced. To pretend his entire focus was on that piece of fir. The planter's son must not sense anything amiss.

In his mind's eye, the wood became Master Cyrus's face. Raising the ax, the lad swung with every ounce of his might, and CRACK! That piece of wood split right down the middle!

"It's about time you figured it out," Master Cyrus fussed. "Now keep doin' that. You're gonna have to work fast to make up for the lost time."

Callum sucked in a deep breath.

"What was that for, red-leg?" Master Cyrus questioned. "That wasn't a disrespectful sigh I heard, was it?"

"No, sir. I'm just tired."

"That better be all it is. I expect to see a lot of progress by the time I come back to check on you in a little while. Understand?"

"Yes, sir," Callum said.

Master Cyrus adjusted his suspenders and headed back toward the plantation house. As he walked away, Callum split round after round of wood. After half an hour of splitting, he took a break and looked around. In the far distance, Ghazi was tending the field. Thankfully, he was facing the opposite direction from where Callum was working. Other than Ghazi, no one was in sight.

Callum set the ax down. It was now or never. Either way could lead to trouble. Ghazi might hear his feet pounding the field if he ran too fast. If he went too slow, Ghazi might turn around in time to see him going.

With a racing heart, Callum turned his attention to the fence-line, though it was currently out of sight, and made a mad dash toward it. He could only hope no one would see or hear. One thing was for sure; there would be no looking back.

For several minutes everything was a fog. Callum saw, heard, nor felt anything. He couldn't believe he had finally worked up enough courage or stupidity, whichever it was, to make his move.

After running a while more, Callum's left side began to ache. Holding it with one hand, he continued running while trying to breathe in through his nose and out through his mouth. For a few minutes, the lad felt like he would fall over, but determination kept him going. The next thing he knew, from out of nowhere, he had a second wind, enabling him to run as fast as he had when he had first taken off.

Callum ran hard for a good forty-five minutes before finally stopping for air. Doubling over and panting, he was relieved not to hear barking dogs or loud voices coming in his direction. A smile appeared on his face. He had run the first leg of his race, and all was quiet.

A five-minute break was much less than Callum desired but all he could afford. As soon as his heart rate had slowed and his breathing returned to a manageable level, the lad wiped the sweat from his forehead and ran some more. This time he didn't care how bad his side hurt or how shallow his breathing might become; he refused to stop until he got to that fence-line.

The lad might be sore in the morning, but that soreness would be well worth it! Callum McCarthy was on his way to freedom! And when he got it, no one would ever take it away. That he was sure of.

Callum squinted his eyes. Sure enough, he was right! The fence-line and the dirt road behind it were coming into view! Running was becoming more and more difficult, but he didn't have time for another break. He was sure Master Cyrus had found out he was missing by now. If a search party weren't already out looking for him, it would be soon.

Callum just hoped Ghazi hadn't seen which direction he took off in. If he didn't, that would buy him at least a smidgeon of extra time.

CHAPTER TWENTY-NINE
HIDING OUT

Some might view an uprooted pine tree as taking away from a forest's beauty. However, it was a welcome sight in the eyes of a thirteen-year-old newly homeless lad. Callum had curled himself into a ball inside a small hole partially covered by protruding roots.

The lad would have continued his journey to Clement's place, but it was too soon. More than likely, Master Josiah would send folks out to search neighboring plantations. He would have to give them a day or two to complete those searches before making a move.

The thoughts crossing one's mind at times like this are too many to count. Yet there was one that continuously trumped all others — was it even remotely possible that Callum could find a way back to Dublin? It wasn't that the McCarthys were a close-knit family. The lad's father rarely contributed anything to the household income as he spent most of his time in buddies' homes or pubs. And his mother lived in a world all of her own, spending the majority of her time sitting in a chair staring out the window and rarely speaking to anyone around her. As for Callum and his siblings, they did whatever cooking, cleaning, and laundry needed doing. That was pretty much the extent of their relationship. Callum's desire to return to Dublin was not so much because he had a close connection with his family but more so to return a state of semi-normalcy to his life.

Keeping his eyes closed that night proved difficult. Clouds had moved in, blocking out any trace of moonlight. The few visible stars provided only enough light to create eerie shadows around him. Every time Callum moved, another pebble or tree root would make its presence known. Then there were the constant fears of being sneaked up on by a slave catcher, getting attacked by a pack of wolves, and worse. On top of it all, a not-so-gentle breeze was blowing, making comfort an impossibility.

As Callum shivered, the sound of a stone getting kicked across the road caught his ear. Unless he was hearing things, either a person or an animal was close by. Callum wanted to know who or what was down there. At the same time, the slightest movement might give him away.

Listening closer, Callum could better decipher the sound. Someone was on a horse, which was far from usual for that time of night. As the sound drew closer, shadows moved across the tree roots. Whoever was on that horse must have been carrying a lantern.

The horse stopped. "Callum!" a man's voice called. "Callum! Can you hear me?"

The voice sounded familiar, yet Callum was too frightened to respond.

"Callum, this is no place for a lad your age to spend the night! It's dangerous out here, and a storm's moving in!"

Callum knew the man was right on all accounts, but if he were to come out of hiding, he could easily be dragged back to the Gillcrest plantation for the beating of a lifetime. If he survived the whipping, he was confident his workload would drastically increase.

"It's me, Clement!" the voice cried out. "I'm alone! I've been careful. I promise, Callum. Nobody's following me. I won't turn you in!"

Slowly Callum emerged from his safe haven beneath the tree roots. He crawled a few feet on hands and knees until he could see the shadow of a rider on the road. There was only one person in sight, as best as he could tell. "Is that really you, Clement?"

"I knew you were here! I could feel it in my bones!" Clement replied. "Come on down here, lad! Hurry it up."

Cautiously, Callum crept to the road. When he got there, Clement said, "Master Josiah showed up at my parents' place several hours ago, telling us an Irish slave had run off. He described you pretty well and said he had no idea which direction you had taken off in. I waited until my folks were in bed before sneaking out to find you. We can talk later. For now, hop on up here, lad. Let's get you back to my place."

"Yes, sir. And thank you."

"Now listen," Clement said. "Somebody might happen along the road. If they do, we ought to see their lantern far enough in advance that you can jump off my horse and run for the hills. If that happens, I'll continue down the road a piece and come back for you once everything is clear."

"What if they don't have a lantern and they find me with you?" Callum asked.

"If that happens, keep your mouth closed and allow me to handle it."

Callum was on pins and needles. He almost felt safer in the woods alone than on the road, where if any slave catchers were on duty, they were sure to find him. Not only that, but there could be a reward for his return, and there was always the possibility Clement had gotten his eyes on reward money. But he hardly seemed the type, regardless of how selfish the Gillcrests had made him out to be.

Even if Clement was on the level, he had made it clear that his parents would disapprove of a runaway slave being harbored on their property. Spending even one night there could be somewhat risky. Let alone two or three like he had initially planned.

A loud clap of thunder made Callum jump as if he'd been shot. "Whew! That scared me," he said.

"Me too," Clement confessed.

A flash of lightning lit up the sky. Callum was glad he wasn't alone. It sure was kind of his neighbor to put himself out like that.

"Clement," the lad asked nearly twenty minutes into their ride.

"Yes, lad?"

"Why are you doing this for me? It seems like a lot of trouble to go through for somebody you barely even know. I mean, couldn't you get into a lot of trouble over this?"

Clement chuckled, "Trouble's my middle name, lad. I couldn't count the number of switches and tree limbs that got broken across my backside when I was growing up. Not that my folks were abusive. I probably deserved more than I got. But I guess you could say I have a soft heart. What about you, lad? How did you end up at Master Gillcrest's?"

Callum told him the whole story about being kidnapped from his living room floor, making the voyage across the sea, and being auctioned off to the highest bidder – Master Josiah Gillcrest.

"It breaks my heart to see and hear of things like this," Clement said. "Nobody ought to be a slave for life. My aunt and uncle have purchased a few slaves who've secretly shared their stories with me, and they're very similar to yours. My aunt and uncle treat them worse than rabid dogs. If they lived closer or were around more often, I'd do whatever I could to help them escape. But they're not here, and you are. So I'll do what I can for you, lad."

Callum didn't know what to say. He was just thankful good people existed in the world, even in the colonies.

Fortunately, the ride to his neighbor's place was uneventful.

About fifty yards from the central part of the property, Clement brought the horse to a halt. "We've got to be super quiet now. Don't talk, don't sneeze, don't make any noise whatsoever. After I stable the horse, follow me in silence. I'm going to blow the lantern out. Hush now."

CHAPTER THIRTY

MOBS DON'T PLAY NICE

Elevated, masculine voices infiltrated the air. Master Josiah and a group of neighbors had found him, or Master Josiah had hired slave catchers. Whichever way the egg rolled, Callum's freedom was in jeopardy.

"We are not harboring any slaves here, red-leg or smoked Irish," a man said. Not recognizing the voice, Callum assumed it was Clement's father.

Voices were so thunderous Callum had no trouble distinguishing every word. "What about *her?*" Someone asked. "Does your wife know where he is?"

"Leave my wife out of this! She, nor I, would ever do anything to violate the law or cause a ruckus amongst our neighbors."

"What about *your boy?* He's never seen things the way you do, has he? Where is that son of yours anyway? I want to question him!"

"Clement stays out of this!" the man demanded.

With that, tempers erupted. Callum couldn't see anything from his woodshed hideaway but the sounds hitting his ears told him what was happening. The mob had talked long enough. They were searching the property and destroying it as they went.

Callum had to get out of there. But knowing when it was safe to sneak out of the woodshed was next to impossible.

"I've got Clement!' one of the men shouted. In no time, it sounded as though a victory had been won.

"Tell us where that poor-white earth scratching scum is!" one of them hollered.

"He knows!" another one shouted. "Look at his face! Come on, boy, *TALK!* Where did you hide him?"

Callum peeked his head through the door. He couldn't see the men, but he could tell their voices were coming from an area about one hundred yards from the woodshed. Running now might be his safest bet for retaining his freedom. At the same time, fleeing while the mob interrogated his friend didn't feel right.

"Leave him alone!" the father's voice demanded. "Get off my property!"

Within seconds, it sounded like a fight had broken out. "Grab him! Somebody get the rope!"

How had Callum allowed an innocent family to be dragged into such drama? Unfortunately, there was nothing the lad could do to stop what was taking place. After cautiously scanning his surroundings, Callum bolted out of the woodshed, back toward the road.

This time, he wasn't in a fog. He could hear *everything!* "There's the red-leg! After him!" someone shouted.

Callum ran as hard as he could. He had to stay ahead of the mob and get out of their sight. Indeed, at the ripe age of thirteen, the lad could outrun all of them! Or so he hoped.

It sounded like at least one horse was speedily coming upon him. Turning to see how close the rider was, Callum stumbled. In the three seconds it took to hop to his feet, a few fully-grown men surrounded him, a couple of which grabbed his arms and forcefully dragged him toward the house, where other men still had a hold of Clement.

To Callum's shock, Clement didn't deny his involvement. "I'm sorry, Callum," he cried. "I thought you'd be safe here!"

As Callum scanned the crowd, he caught sight of Master Josiah and Master Cyrus.

"What should we do with them, Josiah?" one of the men called out.

"Hand the red-leg over to my son. We'll tend to him back at our plantation. As for Clement, that young rebel needs to be taught not to interfere with other men's property!"

Another fellow, held back by several others, shouted, "You men need to get off our property! Clement had nothing to do with anything!"

His words meant nothing.

Callum struggled to free himself. "Clement was only trying to help me! Let him go!"

The mob listened to no one. One of its members ripped Clement's shirt off as others tied him to a tree. No matter how much Callum or Clement's father begged and demanded

Clement's release, the men were determined to make an example out of the slave rescuer.

Master Josiah took out his whip. It was going to be the first time Callum had seen it used. He watched in horror as Master Josiah brought it back and swung full force. That first lash looked and sounded dreadfully painful. Callum winced as Clement screamed out in agony.

As much as the lad hoped the entire lesson would be taught by one lash, he knew better. The whip was raised high in the air and came crashing down again. Clement yelped like an injured dog. Callum struggled again, trying to free himself to run to Clement's aid, but Master Cyrus had a firm grip on him.

For a few seconds, Callum took his eyes off Master Josiah and Clement and examined the faces of the mob. One man looked angry, another laughed, and a third shook his head. How could so many men fathom it okay to mete out such a cruel punishment to someone whose only crime was providing shelter for a lad in the midst of a storm?

As the whip tore into Clement's flesh yet again, Master Cyrus laughed wickedly. "Just wait, lad!" He squeezed Callum a little tighter. "You'll get to experience that whip yourself before long! You won't be runnin' away again any time soon!"

After ten brutal lashes, the mob dispersed. Master Cyrus forced Callum back into the carriage and held onto him while Master Josiah drove them back to the Gillcrest plantation.

Callum cried the entire way home. Not only was he upset that the mob caught him, but that Clement had been beaten. And that he himself was about to be. The worst part was that evil look Master Cyrus kept giving him. Callum didn't understand it, but he felt like Master Cyrus, whether he was the one dishing out the punishment or not, truly enjoyed the idea of Callum getting beaten to a bloody pulp.

CHAPTER THIRTY-ONE

HUMILIATED

Overcome with fear, Callum trembled as Master Josiah ordered Ghazi and Jonah to peel his shirt off and secure him to the whipping post. After witnessing Clement's agony and seeing the gory mess he became, the lad didn't want to ponder what was about to happen.

Master Cyrus paced back and forth in front of Callum, holding the whip up for the lad and everyone else on the plantation to see. Closing his eyes, Callum wished never to catch another glimpse of that wicked instrument.

Once the lad was secure, Master Josiah spoke harshly, "As you're all aware, yesterday, this foolish red-leg chose to defy me by fleeing the plantation. Thus far, we have *never* had a slave escape and retain his freedom, and *we never will*. Let what you're about to witness serve as a reminder to each of you. Never, under any circumstances, defy your master or his family. The one thing that will be different with Callum's case is this. Most of you aren't aware, but when I purchased this lad, it was to give him to Cyrus when he turned eighteen years of age. In light of the present circumstances, I have decided to make that property transfer effective as of this moment. Callum no longer belongs to me. Therefore, his new master will be the one teaching him a lesson. He's all yours, son. Let him have it!"

Callum cried harder as Master Cyrus slowly passed in front of him one final time with the whip. Unless he was seeing things, the planter's son grinned and winked at him as he passed.

Time stood still as Callum waited for the first lash. He could hear Master Cyrus getting himself and the whip in position. He remembered Jonah warning him not to even think about running away. And how Ghazi brought it to his attention that Jonah had been trying to watch out for him. It was too late. Far too late.

Thinking he had just swung, Callum lurched forward and winced, only to find out it had only been his imagination. As much as he dreaded what was coming, the lad also hoped Master Cyrus would hurry up and get it over with.

Instead of feeling the whip, he heard Master Cyrus walking closer to him. Suddenly he whispered in his ear, "You are *mine*, you poor-white earth scratching scum. Don't you ever forget it! I'm going to delight in your begging for mercy!"

That did it! Callum decided right then and there that he would not show any sign of being affected by that whip, regardless of how many times he got hit. He refused to scream, yelp, or plead for sympathy. He would not give Master Cyrus the satisfaction.

Thirty seconds later, Callum heard the same sounds as before. It appeared as though Master Cyrus was getting ready to lay it on him. He gritted his teeth and clenched his fists. When that whip made contact, the lad would pretend he didn't feel a thing, no matter how it felt.

That was a good plan until the whip cracked. Callum screamed louder than he ever had in his life. That whip cut. It stung. Its pain was unlike any he had ever known. Callum tried to yank his hands loose but to no avail. It cut him a second time! So good to pretending it didn't hurt! Callum howled out in pain. "I'm sooooorrrrrry! I'll never run away again! Pleeeeaaaaase, pleeeeaaaaase! I've learned my lesson!"

Callum's legs trembled beneath him. Yes, it had only been two lashes, but the pain was unbearable. He couldn't take more. His body couldn't withstand another lash. Or so he thought before the whip hit again. The lad let out a horrendous scream. Regardless of how much blood he lost and how much he screamed and writhed in pain, the lashes continued raining down on him. Twenty in all. That's what Master Cyrus gave him.

"My father's custom in situations like this is to give the red-leg two days to recover before he returns to the fields. I have no such custom. Callum, you have one hour to regain your strength, and then you'll enter that field and work as you've never worked before."

Callum sobbed as Master Cyrus untied him from the whipping post. His body fell to the ground the moment his hands were no longer secured. He had no strength or expectation of finding freedom. His worst nightmare had come true, and there was nothing he could do about it.

Never did Callum want to be brutalized like that again. For that matter, the lad never wished to see or hear another whipping ever in his life.

Callum began replaying everything that had happened in his mind — dropping the ax and running for the fence-line, hiding under the uprooted pine, and riding Clement's horse to his parents' place later that night. Fast-forwarding several hours, the lad pictured the mob hunting for him, Master Josiah beating Clement for helping him, and lastly, finding himself strapped to that whipping post.

For the first time during the whole ordeal, a flood of humiliation swept over him. Everybody on the plantation knew he had run away and gotten caught. They had all seen him squall like a baby while getting whipped in front of them.

At least he had been brave enough to attempt an escape! Most of them would never have dared try. And those who had, with Caspar being the exception, had only tried once. They had allowed that whip to intimidate them. To make them give up.

Sure, for a few seconds, Callum felt the same way. But not for long. One day, he would find a way off that Gillcrest plantation.

"Cyrus," Master Josiah suddenly called out. "Give me the whip."

Already hurting worse than he knew possible, the fear of getting beaten all over again, this time by Master Josiah, terrified Callum. The lad clenched his teeth and squeezed his eyes shut. He didn't want to see, hear, or feel anything.

"Please don't do this, Father!" Master Cyrus suddenly blurted out. "I know I promised, but I really don't want to go through with this."

Oh! How had Callum forgotten the deal? He wasn't going to get a second whipping. Master Cyrus had one coming to him!

"Do you think Callum wanted to go through with it?"

Master Cyrus released a defeated sigh, "No, sir."

"But he accepted the correction anyway, did he not?"

Sighing a second time, Master Cyrus handed the whip to his father.

Callum would have enjoyed the spectacle had Master Cyrus not severely beaten him moments before. Still, he stayed to watch.

Master Cyrus obediently took his shirt off and placed himself in front of the whipping post, where he waited for his father to secure his arms.

"I'm sorry," Master Josiah said, "but a man's word is a man's word. Our agreement was thirty lashes."

Master Cyrus took a deep breath. "Father, I had forgotten about the deal. When you placed me in charge of the red-leg, I only gave him twenty. Can you please just give me what I gave him?"

"No, Cyrus. That's not what you agreed to. If you chose to go light on your slave, that was your decision. This is mine."

How could Master Josiah say his son had gone easy on him? Callum tried to rise back to his feet but could barely muster enough strength to move an inch. The planter's son was going to take ten more lashes than he did? Surely not!

Callum watched as Master Josiah raised the whip and slammed it against his son's back. Master Cyrus let out a loud groan. How he didn't scream, Callum didn't understand. Four more times, he watched the planter's son have his flesh torn open without uttering a word. Callum wasn't even the one being hit, but he could feel the agony of each and every lash.

Beginning with the sixth blow, Master Cyrus no longer maintained his composure. He squalled every bit as loudly as Callum had moments before. The whip came back again.

Callum couldn't stand it. He closed his eyes and covered his ears. No matter how cruel Master Cyrus had been, he couldn't bear to witness any more of what was unfolding. Not that covering his ears actually blocked out the cracking whip or the pain-filled cries continuously escaping his master's lips.

The beating seemed as though it would never end. A little more than halfway into it, Callum began bawling like a baby. No one, slave or free, should ever face such brutal treatment.

CHAPTER THIRTY-TWO

ANOTHER LOSS

Since becoming the property of Master Cyrus a few weeks ago, Callum was beginning to forget what a good night's sleep was. Every night it seemed he either went to bed on an empty stomach, with a fat lip or black eye, or with an intense craving to rip his new master apart limb by limb.

Missing so much sleep was affecting both the lad's body and mind. That's what convinced him to give the whole Sunday service thing another try. Callum slipped in a few minutes after the service had begun. The congregation was in the middle of singing and clapping to another song he'd never heard of. The lad clapped his hands along with them, even though he had practically no idea what they were singing about.

After the song, Jonah said, "Glad you decided to join us, Callum. Would you like to share something good the Lord's done for you?"

Callum hated nothing more than being put on the spot. What had the Lord done for him? That was a tough one! "The Lord, um... He... uh... I don't know what to say."

Jonah chuckled, "That's okay, lad. Let me tell you all something He's done for me! When Callum ran away, I didn't want to tell anybody, but I felt like I had been foolish to keep workin' this plantation. Like maybe Callum was right. Like I should have taken off in search of my own freedom. When the Gillcrests brought him back, I was filled with hatred. Not because the lad returned but because my hopes of freedom disappeared when Callum couldn't get away. I had mixed feelings when he got that whipping. A part of me thought it served the little fellow right. Another part of me wanted to lead all of you in an uprising. Oh, but I got to praying. I got to seeking my Lord and Savior. And let me tell you what He did! He got to dealin' with my heart. He told me I need to be content with what I have and with where I am. He gave me that kind of peace that passes all understanding. Oh, I want to praise God for taking that bitterness out of my soul!"

"Thank you, Jesus!" Caspar shouted. "He's been good to me too! But nothing like that! Let me tell you. A couple of afternoons ago, I was stacking firewood when I felt somethin' on my neck. I went to brush it off and come to find out it was a spider. One of those big, hairy types. You all know how much I hate spiders! Trying not to panic, I knocked that thing off of me. I stomped on it when it hit the ground, only to find out that spider was pregnant. All kinds of baby spiders came running out! I started trying to stomp all of them at one time."

Caspar laughed, "You should have seen how fast my legs were moving. I was stomping those little babies left and right. When I squished the guts out of the last one and got to a place where I could breathe normally again, my mind went back to that story Jonah shared with us about ole King David dancin' before the Lord. I know I wasn't really dancing before the Lord, but somehow it put that image in my head. And I started praising the Lord by dancin' around. If anybody had seen me, they would have thought I was a crazy man. But I'll tell you what. I had a great time out there with God. Just thanking

Him for helping me get those spiders before they could get me!"

Callum chuckled. He wished he could have been there to see that. It sounded like Caspar was as fond of spiders as he was of snakes.

After a few more people shared their stories, it was time for that exciting part. That part where ole Jonah said he would share a word from the Good Book, even though there still weren't any books laying around.

"There's a book of the Bible called Hebrews. And in the thirteenth chapter of that book, in the eighth verse, it says, 'Jesus Christ the same yesterday, and to day, and for ever.' What a wonderful thought that is! The same Jesus that hanged upon that cross and asked God the Father to forgive the very men who had mocked Him, spit upon Him, beat Him, and put those nails through his hands is the same Jesus that's sitting up in Heaven on the right-hand side of God the Father. He's the same Jesus that serves as the intercessor between man and God. The Creator hasn't changed. He's still just as longsuffering as He ever was. He's still just as kind. Just as gentle. And just as just. Oh, what a Savior! Aren't you thankful Jesus never changes?"

Those folks started shouting their Amens and Hallelujahs again. Callum looked at all of them like they were out of their minds. Somehow, he doubted this whole Sunday service thing would do anything to improve his mental state.

Jonah's sermon dragged on for nearly two hours. As a matter of fact, it was still going on when Master Cyrus stormed over and interrupted. "Enough of this nonsense," he barked. "Callum, I've got a job for you to do. Come with me."

The other slaves grew silent. Everyone knew Sunday was supposed to be their day off.

"What are you waiting for?" Master Cyrus shouted.

Callum peacefully stood and followed him away from the church service. "You've been lookin' way too puny as of late. I don't think I've been workin' you hard enough! So, I've made a decision. No more Sundays off. And you're gonna start workin' two hours past dark, every night."

The thirteen-year-old could barely believe his ears. He needed more rest, not less.

"The barn needs mucked. The chimney needs swept. It smells like you haven't bathed or washed your clothes for a couple of months. You've got two hours to get all of that done, and then I'll give you the remainder of your assignments for the day."

CHAPTER THIRTY-THREE

SURPRISE VISIT

Sometimes, as Darcy always said, anger floats truth to the surface.

Master Cyrus was livid. About what, Callum wasn't sure. But the words spewing from his mouth were hair-raising. Callum couldn't make out what he was saying, but he knew they were dark.

Suddenly, Master Cyrus locked his eyes on Callum. "What are you starin' at?"

"I'm sorry, sir. I thought you were talking to me."

"I wasn't saying anything to anybody. Get back to carrying that firewood, red-leg!"

"Yes, sir," Callum said, scooping up another armful.

Master Cyrus charged at him and knocked the wood out of his arms. "I've told you before. Don't give me those dirty looks!" Master Cyrus backhanded the lad before knocking him to the ground. "Don't even glance in my direction for the rest of the day. Get to work!"

As Callum carried and stacked wood, he heard Master Cyrus repeatedly talking to himself. Every now and then, he could make out a sentence or two such as, "I don't care what anybody else thinks. There's nothin' wrong with me."

Callum didn't know what was going on. Never had he seen anyone behave so irrationally. Was the young master drunk? Had he fallen and hit his head on something?

"Stupid, stupid, stupid!" Master Cyrus muttered. "How could I be so stupid?"

Callum chuckled as he stacked more wood against the plantation house. At least that last question made sense. Callum had often wondered the same thing about Master Cyrus. How could he be so stupid?

With a slew of gibberish rushing out of his mouth, Master Cyrus stormed toward the barn. Callum didn't know where he was going, nor did he care. He was just thankful he could now turn his back without fearing an attack from behind.

After two more hours of stacking, Mistress Rosanna appeared out of nowhere. Tears flowed down her face, and she was fanning herself with her hand. "Have you seen Master Cyrus within the last thirty minutes or so?"

"No, ma'am," Callum said.

Callum had never seen Mistress Rosanna look so upset before. "Everything okay, ma'am?"

Shaking her head, she fled in a hurry.

Ten minutes later, Master Josiah met Callum just outside the plantation house. "Where's Cyrus?" he asked.

"I haven't seen him for a couple of hours," Callum replied.

"You're not lying to me, are you?"

"No, sir. The last time he was by here, he was in a foul mood. He was heading toward the barn."

"If you're lying to me, I'll see to it you get another lashing," Master Josiah warned.

"I'm not lying."

"And if I find out you've done anything to hurt him, I'll take your life with my bare hands!"

Did Master Josiah seriously think a thirteen-year-old was capable of killing a seventeen-year-old? Sure, he had thought about it several times but actually doing it was something else altogether. Instead of being upset at such an allegation, Callum took it as a compliment. If Master Josiah thought he was strong enough to take out Master Cyrus, maybe he was.

Wait a minute! If Mistress Rosanna couldn't find Master Cyrus, and Master Josiah thought Callum might have hurt him, was there a possibility something had happened to his young master? That could be the kind of break Callum was waiting for! If he didn't have a master, would that make him free? The lad wasn't sure how that worked, but it was a thought nonetheless!

Callum carried several more loads of firewood before Master Josiah returned. This time he had a stranger with him. "Sheriff, this is Callum McCarthy, the red-leg you were asking about."

Callum found himself trembling. He had never seen a sheriff before. But he had heard enough talk to know what one was. That man looked every bit as mean as Master Cyrus. The sheriff gave Callum a once-over.

"Hold out your hands, lad."

Squinting his eyes in anticipation of being hit, Callum cautiously put both hands out in front of him.

"Flip them over. I want to see your palms."

Callum complied.

"Where did you sneak out to last night?"

"I didn't go anywhere," Callum said.

"Don't lie to the man, Callum," Master Josiah said.

"I'm not lying. I stayed in my cabin all night."

"Josiah, if you'll excuse us. I'd like to have Callum show me his cabin. Is that okay with you?"

"No problem," Master Josiah said. "Let me know if you need me. I'm going to keep searching for Cyrus."

On the way to Callum's cabin, the sheriff went on with his line of questioning. "Callum, I understand you ran away a while back, and Clement Alloway hid you in his parents' woodshed. Is that correct?"

"Yes, sir."

The sheriff jotted something down on a piece of paper. "Have you seen Clement since that morning when they found you?"

Callum shook his head. "No, sir."

Raising one eyebrow, the sheriff said, "Not even one time?"

"No, sir," Callum repeated.

The sheriff appeared doubtful. "How did you feel when you got caught? Did you think it was Clement's fault somehow?"

"No, sir. Clement did me a favor. He tried to help me escape."

"And just why exactly were you trying to escape?"

Callum dropped his eyes to the ground.

"What are you not telling me, lad?"

"May I speak freely, sir? Without you telling anybody what I'm telling you?"

"Absolutely, lad."

"Being here scares me. Master Cyrus is always looking for excuses to beat me. Master Josiah has threatened to kill me with his bare hands. There are pictures of kids in that house that nobody will talk about. I found some graves —"

The sheriff cut him off. "You found *graves*? On this property?"

"Yes, sir. And Master Cyrus told me they belonged to some animals they used to have. But I dug one up, and —" Callum began to cry again. "It was a human! I think all the graves are of humans, and I don't want somebody to kill me!"

CHAPTER THIRTY-FOUR

GOODBYE, GOOD RIDDANCE

Being pinned against the wall by a potential murderer was not necessarily the highlight of Callum's week. "Why did you tell the sheriff about those graves?" Master Cyrus asked.

Callum was shaking like a leaf. The sheriff wasn't supposed to tell anybody. Now, his life was in danger. "I'm sorry. I wasn't trying to get anybody in trouble," Callum said.

"Too bad. You did get somebody in trouble. That somebody is you. Come with me, now!"

Without getting appropriately dressed, Callum was marched outside and handed a shovel. "We're heading out to those graves right now. You're gonna dig up every last one of 'em. And you're gonna move 'em before that sheriff has a chance to come back out here pokin' around. And when he asks why there's so much soft dirt out there, we're gonna tell him we know nothin' about it. Understood?"

"Yes, sir," Callum said nervously.

Master Cyrus grumbled under his breath again, "They're already tryin' to bag me for one murder. I'm not gonna make it easier for them to charge me with more."

Callum didn't like the sound of that. He wished Master Cyrus hadn't still been alive. Or at least that he hadn't come out of hiding. The planter's son shoved him. "Hurry up. You've got a lot of work ahead of you."

To Callum's shock, the sheriff suddenly stepped out from behind a large oak tree. "Look what we have here!" he said. "What's going on here, Cyrus?"

Master Cyrus snatched the shovel from Callum's hand and drew it back. "Back off, sheriff," he demanded, slowly moving toward him.

Feeling like someone was sneaking up behind them, Callum turned just in time to watch Master Josiah run upon and tackle Master Cyrus to the ground.

The sheriff wasted no time moving in and putting Master Cyrus in handcuffs. "You're coming with me," he said.

"Father! How could you?" Master Cyrus cried out. "Don't let him take me! Please!"

Master Josiah was the element of calm. "If you're innocent, it will be proven, son."

The sheriff glared at Master Josiah, "I'll be back out here in the morning. Do not permit anyone to touch any of those graves under any circumstances," he ordered.

"There aren't any graves on this property that I'm aware of," Master Josiah said. "But we won't do anything to interfere with your investigation." Turning to Callum, he added, "I know what you're thinking, and you're wrong. Just because Cyrus is getting locked up doesn't mean you're free. You are a life-long servant on the Gillcrest plantation, and that's how it will stay. Get back to your cabin and get some sleep."

How did everyone always know what Callum was thinking? That's what he wanted to know.

Silently, the lad complied with the directions and did an about-face. That's when he saw it. Somehow Master Cyrus had dropped his pocket watch. Callum glanced over his shoulder. The sheriff, Master Josiah, and Master Cyrus were too busy paying attention to each other to notice what he was doing. The lad quickly scooped up the watch and dropped it in his pocket. If Master Cyrus wanted that old thing, he should have kept a better eye on it.

Callum hurriedly made his way back to his quarters. He could hardly wait to get a close look at that watch. When he got there, however, he was startled to find Mistress Rosanna waiting inside. "Callum," she said. "I'll make this as short as I can. No one must know I was ever here."

"Yes, ma'am," Callum said.

"No matter what happens from this point forward, I don't want you giving that sheriff any more information about things you find or see on our property. Do you understand me?"

"Yes, ma'am."

"Don't forget I'm the one who makes most of your meals."

"I won't forget, ma'am."

"Good. Now you stop flapping those gums about everything you know. I was never here.

I never said anything to you about anything at all."

Callum wasn't ashamed of telling the sheriff about those mounds of dirt. If anything, he was glad he had done it. Now, he would get a chance to find out if only the one mound had a body in it or if all of them did. It was only a matter of time.

As Callum laid down for the second time that night, Master Cyrus's words echoed around in his head.

What murder were they trying to charge him with? And why was the sheriff under the impression Callum had sneaked off in the middle of the night? Something wasn't adding up. Nobody on the plantation was missing, not that Callum had noticed or heard about. Who else could be dead?

Callum tried to rack his brain. He couldn't think of anybody Master Cyrus had recently feuded with. Nobody he was jealous or afraid of. Maybe somebody had caught him doing something wrong, and he killed them so they couldn't talk?

Rocking back and forth on his bed, Callum tried to fall asleep. The faster he closed his eyes, the faster the morning would come. And the quicker the morning came, the quicker he would have the answers he longed for. When that ole sheriff came back around, more information would arrive with him. Callum just knew it.

Unfortunately, telling yourself you need to go to sleep and actually doing so isn't necessarily the same thing. Every time the lad closed his eyes, an invisible spring popped them back open, and he again found himself looking for patterns on the ceiling and walls.

Callum's eyelids were beginning to hurt. How many nights in a row could he go without a decent night's rest? He sure hoped that sheriff would get to the bottom of everything. Even if it didn't give him his sleep back, it would at least calm his nerves.

Callum got out of bed and paced the floor. The more he thought about it, there was only one person he could think of that Master Cyrus may have killed. But why?

CHAPTER THIRTY-FIVE

MAJOR CHANGES COMING

Callum had no idea Mistress Rosanna could be so aggressive. "You're making a big mistake, sheriff!" she shouted. "You can't arrest my husband without evidence!"

Her husband? Callum was beyond confused. Last night Master Josiah helped the sheriff arrest Master Cyrus. Now he was in trouble too? Maybe the lad didn't hear that quite right.

Quietly, he stepped out of his cabin to see what was happening.

"I'm mighty sorry, Mistress Rosanna. But after speaking with Cyrus and questioning your husband, I need to keep them both in my office until I complete a thorough investigation. I'll be back later today to oversee the excavation of the gravesites."

Mistress Rosanna looked as though she could spit fire. "You better not let anything happen to either of them!" she said firmly. "You won't get away with this, sheriff!"

Mistress Rosanna eased herself into a chair on the porch as the sheriff hauled her husband off the property. Callum and all of the other slaves rushed to her side. "Everything's going to be alright, Mistress Rosanna," Amelia said.

"I'm not so sure," Mistress Rosanna replied. "I fear we're in for major changes around here."

"What do you mean?" Amelia asked.

"I'm not going to say any more than I have to. But I wouldn't be surprised if neither Josiah nor Cyrus ever come back alive." Mistress Rosanna let out a long sigh. "Amelia, I'm not sure I can handle cooking breakfast this morning. Would you take over in the kitchen for me?"

"Yes, ma'am. I'll get right on it. You just sit right here and take it easy for a spell."

Callum was pleased. Life would be much easier without either of the Gillcrest men on the premises. Mistress Rosanna had a heart of gold. That woman wouldn't take a whip to anybody, no matter what they did or didn't do. Callum was sure of that. "Would you like me to set the table, ma'am?"

"Yes, Callum. Please do," she said.

That was a perfect example of what Callum liked about Mistress Rosanna. She spoke to him like a human being. She asked him to do things instead of simply barking out commands.

The lad refused to invest too much time into thinking about how much nicer everything would be with the significant changes Mistress Rosanna had referred to. If he had learned anything in the short thirteen years of his existence, it was that whenever things seemed to be going well, something terrible would soon follow. More than likely, Mistress Rosanna would be wrong. Worst case scenario, Master Josiah wouldn't come back alive, and his son would. If Master Cyrus ran the whole plantation, they would all be in a world of hurt!

Inside, Callum found out he wasn't the only one whose mind was reeling. "I don't even know what to think right now," Amelia said in somewhat of a whisper. "I'm upset for Mistress

Rosanna. I can't imagine how I would feel if somebody stole Jonah from me. But for the rest of us, this might be the biggest blessing we've ever known."

That was the most Amelia had ever spoken to Callum. He tried to keep the conversation going. "What I don't understand is why, if Mistress Rosanna is such a good person, she would have married somebody like Master Josiah. Or why she would have raised a son that turned out like Master Cyrus?"

"Watch your tongue, lad," Amelia snapped. "Mistress Rosanna has been nothing but kind to you and everybody else on this plantation. I won't listen to you speak so poorly of her when she's not here to defend herself."

There went that idea! How was it okay for Amelia to say negative things about Master Josiah and Master Cyrus but not for him to make similar comments regarding Mistress Rosanna? Adults could be so difficult to understand.

As out of character as it was for him, Callum did not apologize. Instead, he set the rest of the table in silence before proceeding outside. The lad wasn't sure where the other slaves had disappeared to. But Mistress Rosanna was still sitting in her chair, looking distraught.

Callum sat on the ground next to her without uttering a word.

She sat quietly for a moment before questioning him, "I heard what you said in there. Is there a reason you doubt I'm as good of a person as people think I am?"

Callum had no idea how to respond to such a question. His first instinct was to lie. To pretend he had no idea what she was talking about. But she did ask, and nobody was around who could give him a lashing if he answered in a way they thought rude or disrespectful. "I don't know," Callum said. "There was this lady named Darcy who used to take care of me when I was younger. She always said you could tell a lot about a person by who they choose to marry. I don't mean any disrespect, but your husband has a temper. And —"

"That's quite enough, Callum," Mistress Rosanna said. "I understand where you're coming from. But as Amelia told you inside, it's not a good idea to badmouth folks when they aren't in our presence."

"I guess you're right," the lad said. "From now on, I'll be more careful how I respond to questions."

Mistress Rosanna raised her eyebrows but didn't speak. Callum knew his point had been made.

A few minutes later, the other slaves approached the house. Somehow, they always knew when it was mealtime.

"Coming inside?" Ghazi asked Mistress Rosanna.

She shook her head slowly, "I don't feel up to eating breakfast. You all go ahead without me. And don't forget to say your prayers!"

Callum followed the other slaves inside and took a seat. Jonah asked the blessing in a rather unusual manner, "Dearest Father in Heaven, sometimes I think You must sit up there scratching Your beard wondering if we are ever going to fully trust You. Lord, we don't always understand why You allow things to happen the way You do. But we know You are the master planner. Whether You choose to allow Master Josiah and Master Cyrus to rejoin us here on this beautiful plantation or whether You choose to keep them away, we are not going to complain or fear but to have hearts of gratitude. Lord, we ask You to bless this food and bless Amelia for preparing it for us. We ask these things in the name of Jesus. And all God's people said —"

All of the slaves answered with a hearty "Amen."

CHAPTER THIRTY-SIX

THE TRUTH COMES OUT

The sheriff brought in a host of volunteers to excavate the dirt mounds, and Mistress Rosanna was anything but happy about it. "Never in my life have I seen or even heard of anything so ridiculous!" she complained. "Turning neighbors against neighbors. Look at you!"

Callum was surprised Mistress Rosanna or the sheriff hadn't ordered the slaves to dig up the mounds themselves. But the sheriff said there were specific protocols he needed to follow, and no one on the plantation was permitted to touch anything he was investigating.

While his crew dug, the sheriff pulled different slaves aside and asked questions. Callum wondered what was going on. Eventually, he found out. "Callum, I know we've already talked," the sheriff said. "But I'm now at a place where I can share some information with you. First of all, has anyone told you about Clement Alloway?"

Callum was afraid of that. "I haven't heard anything. No, sir."

"He's no longer living. I can't give out specific details of his death as the investigation is still unfolding, but I will tell you his death appears to have been a homicide."

Callum looked confused.

"Homicide? You know, murder?" the sheriff continued.

The news hit so fast that Callum had trouble processing it. Of all people to be killed, why the one and only friend the lad had? "You think Master Josiah and Master Cyrus were both involved? Is that why you arrested them?"

"I can't answer that question just yet. Callum, I need to know if you've seen or heard anything that would make you suspect anyone on this plantation of being capable of committing homicide? Not just in regards to Clement."

"Sheriff, I told you before. Master Josiah has threatened to kill me with his bare hands. Master Cyrus has beaten me on multiple occasions. Both of them have violent tempers. Since I've been here, I haven't seen anyone killed, but Clement told me about some suspicions he had, and Ghazi said Jonah's son was killed."

The sheriff jotted down a few notes, "What else should I know?"

"Well," Callum said. "I'm not sure if this is important or not. But one time, Jonah told me one of Master Josiah's sons, I believe his name was Master Oliver, had disappeared several years ago. He claimed Master Cyrus told his father the lad had run away and insisted Jonah knew his whereabouts. He said Master Josiah asked him about it, and when he insisted he knew nothing, they gave him a severe whipping for it. His back still has scars from that whipping. What if his son didn't really run away? And Master Josiah and Master Cyrus teamed up against Jonah so things would look less suspicious?"

Shortly after Callum gave his statements, more people from neighboring plantations showed up. It's incredible how fast word travels. Callum had no idea so many people lived within such easy traveling distance of the Gillcrests. He guessed at least fifteen visitors were present. He recognized a few as being a part of the mob responsible for Clement's beating.

After an exhausting day of watching, listening, and worrying, Callum was almost relieved when the sheriff told everyone to quiet down for an announcement. "Folks, I'm about to share news many of you will find disturbing. If you have small children present, please be aware that the information I'm about to disclose is of a brutal nature. If you don't want your little ones hearing this, you may want to cover their ears at this time."

Callum looked around. A few young children were present, but no one covered their ears. Things grew more tense than Callum could have ever imagined.

"Based on testimonies of witnesses and suspects, and taking into consideration the evidence gathered in the past twenty-four hours, it is apparent that Clement's death was not an accident. He was murdered."

Sighs of disbelief filled the crowd.

"Furthermore," the sheriff continued, "the mounds we have been uncovering contained skeletal remains, and those remains are human. It's abundantly clear that none of these people died of natural causes. Each was murdered."

The sheriff paused. He looked nervous, as did the rest of the crowd. "At this time, we only have two suspects," he continued. "I believe either Josiah Gillcrest or his son Cyrus is guilty of intentionally taking Clement's life. There is a possibility both were involved."

Mistress Rosanna cried, "No! No! You don't know what you're saying! My husband nor my baby would ever do such a thing!"

The sheriff motioned for her to quiet down. "A hearing will be held in my office tomorrow morning. Due to space limitations, only residents of the Alloway and Gillcrest plantations will be permitted to attend the trial. The verdict will be presented to the public as soon as possible."

CHAPTER THIRTY-SEVEN

THE TRIAL BEGINS

Mr. Alloway gave Callum an evil glare as he and his wife passed in front of the slaves from the Gillcrest plantation. That look was one Callum had seen before. It said Callum was responsible for what had happened to their son. Callum had to fight back his own tears. He wished he could have traded places with Clement.

Lowering his eyes to the floor, Callum wished the trial could be over or that he could have stayed at the plantation while it was underway.

The sheriff's office was eerily quiet for a few minutes as everyone got into their places.

Eventually, the sheriff broke the silence, "As you all know, we are here today to determine who is guilty of murdering Clement Alloway as well as those buried on the Gillcrest plantation.

"I apologize for not having enough chairs for everyone to sit. Please feel free to stand or sit on the floor. We will make every effort to get through these proceedings as quickly as possible."

Callum made eye contact with different people in the room. Master Cyrus's face was pasty white except for the purple bags under his eyes. Rubbing his hands together, the planter's son nervously stared out the only window in the sheriff's office. Master Josiah, on the other hand, appeared to be counting the number of people in the room. He looked uncomfortable but nowhere near as afraid as Master Cyrus.

"Things will be done decently and in order," the sheriff continued. "I will question one person at a time. The questioning will continue until I am confident the right party has been found guilty, and then we'll go from there. Let's begin with Mr. William Alloway, the father of the most recently deceased victim, Clement Alloway."

Callum didn't understand legal matters, but it sure didn't seem fitting for the father to go first, if at all. It would seem more proper for those suspected of the crime to go first. Or for the sheriff to ask for potential witnesses to come forward. If he were an adult, and if he had his freedom, he probably would have said so. But under the circumstances, the lad kept quiet.

"Mr. Alloway, it's my understanding that your son had an encounter with Josiah Gillcrest several years back – an encounter that gave him quite the scare. Do you remember Clement reporting unusual happenings on the day you sent him to fetch Rosanna Gilcrest?"

"Yes, sir. I remember it. Last night, I kept replaying Clement's words and my shameful reaction to him over and over again. If only I had listened—" Master Alloway choked back his tears.

"Tell me about that day, Mr. Alloway. What did Clement tell you?"

"Let me back up. My wife was ill. In the past, Rosanna had told us to let her know if we ever needed anything, and she would be right there. With my wife feverish, I took her up on the offer. I told Clement to rush over and bring her to our place as quickly as possible."

Callum listened closely, curious if Mr. Alloway had heard the same story he had. And if he had heard it, he wondered if the man would have the guts to tell the sheriff the complete truth.

"Clement was gone a few hours. He returned, and Rosanna was right behind him in her carriage. She went in and tended to my wife. While she was doing so, I told my boy to go on about his chores. Clement was quieter than usual, but I figured that was because his momma was lying in bed sick, and he feared it was something serious.

"After a while, Rosanna said my wife was on the rebound, and she needed to get back to Josiah and the plantation. As soon as she left, Clement said he needed to talk to me. We went out on the porch, and my boy shared one of those exaggerated stories he was so good at telling. At least, I assumed that's what it was. Claimed Josiah Gillcrest came around his toolshed covered in fresh blood and was somewhat shaken up about something."

"Did Clement see where the blood came from?" the sheriff asked.

"If he did, he didn't say so. Clement told me Mr. Gillcrest asked if he had heard anything unusual. When he said no, Josiah allegedly didn't believe him. He supposedly warned my son not to tell anybody about the blood or their conversation."

"Did you ever talk to Mr. Gillcrest about the allegations your son made?" the sheriff asked.

"No, sir."

"So what did you do after he told you? Just go on about your business as if you hadn't heard anything?"

Mr. Alloway stood in silence for a moment. Callum began to feel like he had gotten Clement's family in trouble. The sheriff's entire line of questioning was based on things he had told him.

"How did you handle the situation, Mr. Alloway?"

"I... I didn't believe him, Sheriff. Honest, I didn't. Had I thought he was telling the truth, I would have gone out there to investigate."

"Is it true, Mr. Alloway, that you were so convinced your son was lying that you gave him a whipping for what he told you?"

Mr. Alloway wiped a tear from his eye. "I did, Sheriff. At that age, every time his mouth opened, another lie seeped out. I had no reason to believe he was speaking the truth."

"At any time that day, or in the days following, did you ever think there was even the slightest chance Clement's story was true? That something tragic had happened at the Gillcrest plantation?

"Not that I recall."

"Then why did you threaten to whip him a second time if he told anybody else about the accusation?"

Now Callum was beginning to understand why Clement's father was being questioned. What kind of father beats his son for potentially witnessing a crime and threatens him not to tell anybody else about it? Callum was beginning to think the sheriff knew something about William Alloway that he hadn't heard about. Surely Clement's father wasn't involved somehow.

Before Mr. Alloway had a chance to respond, the sheriff popped another question, "Were you afraid of getting your neighbor in trouble?"

"Sheriff, you know our family. My wife and I have never meddled in anybody else's affairs, and I was not about to allow my son to start down that path."

"Mr. Alloway," the sheriff said, "If you thought one of your neighbors had committed a crime, would you try so hard to keep the peace that you would consider turning a blind eye? You know, pretend you didn't see anything?"

Mr. Alloway lowered his head. "To be honest, sir, yes. I would."

"If your wife or your son had reason to believe one of your neighbors committed a crime, would you try to keep them quiet to avoid a confrontation?"

"Sheriff, I know it's going to sound horrible when I say this. But yes. Being completely truthful with you, I would insist that no one in my family involve themselves in other people's troubles."

The more Mr. Alloway spoke, the less Callum liked him. He hoped the sheriff felt the same way.

Chapter Thirty-Eight

MISTRESS ROSANNA TESTIFIES

Mistress Rosanna quivered like a leaf when the sheriff announced he was going to question her next. She fanned her face with both hands and, before long, started to gasp for air.

"Get control of yourself, Mistress Rosanna," the sheriff said. "I just need to ask you a few questions, and then I'll move on to somebody else."

"I'm sorry, sheriff. But both my husband and my son are being accused of murder. I'm so upset I can't even think straight."

"I understand," the sheriff said. "But if you want your husband and son to have a fair trial, you must give us your full cooperation. Do you understand?"

"I'll try."

"You better do better than try!" Master Alloway hollered.

The sheriff pounded a fist against his desk. "No more outbursts from Mr. Alloway or anyone else. Anyone who interrupts will be removed from the hearing and will possibly sit through their own trial at a later date."

The tension in the room made Callum nervous. The sheriff wasn't in the mood to take anything off of anybody. The lad had to sneeze but was determined to hold it in. Under no circumstances did he want the sheriff, of all people, upset with him.

"Mistress Rosanna," the sheriff began. "How many children have you given birth to?"

"Eight," she replied in a tearful whisper.

"Of those eight children, how many are still living?"

Mistress Rosanna shrugged her shoulders.

"I can't read shoulders," the sheriff said. "How many of your children are still alive, Mistress Rosanna?"

"I don't know."

Callum gasped. What a stupid answer! It was a good thing he wasn't the sheriff. He'd have called her out on that one for sure. What a low-down, dirty liar!

"Really?" the sheriff asked. "Your son, Cyrus, is here in the room with us today. That's one. Where are the other seven?"

Callum was scared to death, and he wasn't even the person being questioned. Mistress Rosanna didn't seem as if she were in any hurry to give an answer. She locked eyes on Master Cyrus, then on Master Josiah, then on the sheriff, then moved them over to the Alloways. Callum didn't understand why she wasn't speaking.

"Mistress Rosanna, this office is full of people who want answers. Let's not waste their time. Where are your other children?"

"I don't know."

"Maybe that question was too broad for you. Maybe I should ask about one in particular. Where is Oliver?"

A fresh stream of tears trickled down Mistress Rosanna's face.

"Is Oliver alive?" the sheriff asked.

"I haven't seen him in many years."

"That's not what I'm asking, and you know it. The last time you saw Oliver, was he alive?"

Mistress Rosanna closed her eyes and held them that way as she said, "The last time I saw Oliver, he was... yes, he was alive."

"And did you last see him before or after your husband grabbed him by the ear and dragged him into the plantation house? Did you last see him alive before or after the slaves heard screaming coming out of that house?"

With her eyes still closed, Mistress Rosanna fanned her face again, "I can't say."

"You can't say? Meaning, you don't remember?"

"I just... can't say," Mistress Rosanna replied. "I'm sorry."

Up until Mistress Rosanna was being questioned, Callum had always held her in high esteem. But now? No way! He hoped the sheriff would force her to talk, even if that meant hitching her to a whipping post and beating the truth out of her.

But he didn't. "Okay, Rosanna," the sheriff said. "Let's move on. Has Cyrus ever been violent toward any of your other children?"

Mistress Rosanna opened her eyes and looked around the room for a few seconds. Then, just before speaking, she shut them again. "Cyrus is all boy," she said.

"All boy? What do you mean by that, Mrs. Gillcrest? Do you think it's normal for boys to physically assault their siblings?"

"I'm not sure what you're talking about."

"Rosanna, it's no secret that Cyrus has a bad temper. Some might even say he enjoys seeing others writhe in pain. Why might that be? What has he seen, heard, or experienced that might have led to his deriving pleasure from acts of violence?"

Without warning, Mistress Rosanna's eyes sprung open as wide as saucers. "Who do you think you are, Sheriff? My baby does not like seeing others in pain. He doesn't have a violent nature at all! He's a good lad, and everybody here knows it! Cyrus is handsome, hard-working, respectful to his father and me, and he would do anything for anybody. How dare you attack his character this way!"

"Mrs. Gillcrest, I realize I would be breaking protocol to begin questioning slaves here at this trial, but I'm not above it. You can either be honest with me, or I'll have to make things a lot more uncomfortable for you and your family.

You know I'm not attacking Cyrus's character. What if I just ask some yes and no questions. Would that be easier for you?"

"Yes, sir," she nodded.

"Perfect. Does Cyrus, at least on occasion, have difficulty controlling his anger?"

Mistress Rosanna nodded, "Yes, sir."

"How about your husband? Does he have a bad temper?"

"No."

The sheriff scratched his chin. "How about you? Does anger ever get the best of you?"

"No. Never," Mistress Rosanna insisted.

"Are you aware of anyone in your family intentionally taking the life of another human being, whether related to you or not?"

Mistress Rosanna shook her head, "No. Not that I could say."

"Here we go again," the sheriff said. "What do you mean 'not that I could say.' Are you afraid of somebody in this room?"

"No. I'm not afraid. I just can't say. That's all."

There was nothing keeping that woman from telling what she knew. Callum, the sheriff, and everybody else in that room knew it. It's not that she couldn't say. She had information and was refusing to share it. Where was that whipping post?

CHAPTER THIRTY-NINE

IDENTIFY THE ITEMS

The sheriff excused himself for a moment, walked into another room, and returned with a small rectangular object mysteriously wrapped in a blanket. "Folks, I have proof here that someone on the Gillcrest plantation is a cold-blooded killer. Before I present the evidence, I would like all those who are currently standing to be seated on the floor. All with the exception of Josiah and Cyrus Gillcrest. I would like the two of them to be brought to the front of the room and to stand over here where I, and those watching the proceedings, can clearly see their facial expressions.

Callum's curiosity was getting to him, but he sat patiently as instructed. Hopefully, the sheriff wouldn't pull anything bloody out from under that blanket.

Once everyone was in position, the sheriff said, "Josiah Gillcrest, do you have any idea what kind of evidence I might be about to present?"

"No, sir."

"How about you, Cyrus? Any guesses?"

"Did it come from the toolshed?"

"You're on the right track. Why don't you go ahead and tell us what it is before I pull it out?"

"It's a box of items belonging to my brothers and sisters."

A box in the toolshed? The same one Callum had snooped in? He knew something wasn't right about that box. The lad couldn't believe he had been so close to solving the mystery of those dirt mounds on his own!

The sheriff left no time for dwelling on those thoughts, though. "How did the items end up in this crate, Cyrus?"

"I don't know."

"How do you know about the box then?"

"I found it."

"You found it, where?"

Master Cyrus chuckled awkwardly, "On the ground, halfway between our house and the toolshed."

"I'm assuming this is an area where many people travel on a daily basis?"

"Yes, sir."

"And how do you suppose the container got there?"

"I don't know, sir."

What was with the Gillcrests and their determination not to answer questions? What a waste of time! Callum was getting annoyed. Master Cyrus either collected those items himself and was lying about finding the box, or he knew who put the things there and was concealing the truth for whoever it was. Either way, the facts were going to come out. He might as well just flap those gums and get everything out in the open.

Apparently, the sheriff was growing irritated with Master Cyrus as well. "Josiah?" he asked. "Do you know anything about this box or its contents?"

"No, sir. This is the first I've heard of it."

The sheriff stood in silence for a moment. Callum could only assume that was to afford either of the Gillcrest men an opportunity to change their stories before he continued his line of questioning.

When neither spoke up, the sheriff continued, "In that case, I'm going to remove the blanket and open the crate. Everybody ready?"

Callum glanced around the room, trying to read faces, as did the sheriff. He wasn't sure he believed Master Cyrus simply happened upon the container. Nor was he confident Master Josiah had never seen or even heard about it before. But in the event Master Cyrus was telling the truth, somebody else would have to have placed that box there in plain sight. A murderer would be foolish to leave his evidence where it was sure to be found. Unless, of course, he wanted to be caught.

"Josiah," the sheriff said, "Would you mind telling us about these items? What are they? Or to whom do they belong?"

Mistress Rosanna began sobbing. "No, no, no!" she cried. "I don't want to see this!"

The sheriff pounded his fist against his desk. "I realize this is disturbing, Mistress Rosanna, but we have to present all of the facts in this case in order for the trial to be just. Now, Josiah, please tell me and the other folks here in the room about these items."

Master Josiah took a deep breath as he gazed into the box.

"Do you recognize the items?"

"Yes, sir," Master Josiah said. "Each of them belongs to one of our children."

"And which item belongs to Cyrus?"

Master Josiah shook his head, "None of them, Sheriff."

"And why do you suppose there are items here from all of your other children, but there's nothing here that belongs to Cyrus?"

Master Josiah raised his eyes and bore them into Master Cyrus. "I don't know, Sheriff. To be honest, I don't see anything that belonged to Oliver, either. But like I said, I've never seen this box before. If Cyrus were the only one who didn't have any personal possessions in the box, I would say that would mean Cyrus had collected these items from his siblings. I'm not saying he killed anybody. But it would only make sense that if he were collecting items belonging to his brothers and sisters, none of his own possessions would be in this box."

"Cyrus," the sheriff asked, "Is your father correct about why none of your belongings are here? Somewhere along the line, did you begin stashing your siblings' belongings in this crate for some reason?"

"No, sir. When I found the box, all I did was look inside. I swear on my brother's grave I had nothing to do with this."

"On your brother's grave?" the sheriff asked. "Just where is your brother's grave?"

Master Cyrus and Master Josiah exchanged challenging scowls with one another, "It was just a figure of speech."

"Are you sure about that?"

"Positive, sir."

Callum could tell the sheriff wasn't buying Master Cyrus's story. Who would? All his brothers and sisters were gone, and each had a belonging taken from them. This case was getting easier to crack by the moment. Callum wished they'd stop the proceedings and just get down to business. Why couldn't they just declare Master Cyrus guilty and go from there?

Unfortunately for Callum, the sheriff was a man of his word. He was not about to make a decision until he was sure he was making the right one. "And you are one-hundred percent certain you did not place any of those items in the box?"

"Yes, Sheriff."

"Do you have any idea who did?"

"No. It could have been anybody."

"How about you, Josiah? You've told us a couple of times you had never seen this crate before now. You suggested it was possible Cyrus had collected all of these items. Other than mere speculation, do you have any reason to believe it was him?"

"No, sir."

"Do you suspect anyone else of having anything to do with that box?"

"No, sir. Nobody that comes to mind anyway."

CHAPTER FORTY

AN ADMISSION OF GUILT

With the Gillcrest men still standing in the front of the room, the sheriff turned up the heat. "Gentlemen, we need to address another matter, and it's regarding the day Cyrus here was placed under arrest. As a reminder to everyone here, I was conducting an investigation on the Gillcrest plantation. I caught Cyrus Gillcrest instructing one of his slaves to dig up all of the graves and move the bodies. Furthermore, he told the lad to lie to me if I asked any questions. "Cyrus, why don't you tell everybody what happened when I came out of hiding and asked what was going on."

The planter's son let out a sigh, "I warned you to back off."

"Did you only use words, or did you try to intimidate me somehow?

Master Cyrus lowered his voice. "I'm sorry, Sheriff. I shouldn't have done it."

"Tell them what you did."

Master Cyrus shifted his weight from one leg to the other and stuck his hands in his pockets. Looking at his feet, he said, "I picked up a shovel and acted as though I was going to hit him with it if he didn't leave."

"Hit or kill me with it?" the sheriff asked.

"Hit you. But I wasn't really going to do it, Sheriff. I was just trying to scare you."

"Your father didn't think that was the case, did you, Josiah?"

"No, sir," Master Josiah replied before looking at those seated in front of him. "I tackled Cyrus to prevent him from attacking the sheriff."

"Cyrus," the sheriff continued, "You killed your siblings, didn't you?"

Callum nearly stopped breathing on that one. What a direct hit! If only Master Cyrus would confess, they could all go home and call it a day.

Too bad Master Cyrus shook his head.

Without insisting on an audible answer, the sheriff went on, "You kept one small belonging of each of your victims as reminders of your accomplishments?"

Master Cyrus continued shaking his head.

"You even built your own private cemetery and buried your brothers and sisters out there, didn't you? What I don't understand is why. Why did you kill your family?"

With widening eyes, Cyrus yelled, "That's not true! None of it! I never killed anybody except–"

"Now we're getting somewhere," the sheriff said. "You never killed anybody except who?"

For the first time since the trial began, Master Cyrus cried. "Clement not only enabled but aided my slave in escaping."

"So, Clement deserved to die because he helped Callum escape. Is that what you're telling us?"

"If he hadn't been stopped, he would have encouraged more slaves to run away from their plantations."

"So, you took the law into your own hands?"

"I did."

"Murderer!" Mrs. Alloway screamed. He admitted it! Hang him!"

The sheriff punched his desk again. "Let's not be too hasty here, Mrs. Alloway. I need everybody to keep calm until we finish the trial. Cyrus, I need to ask you a few more questions, and I need you to be completely honest with me."

"I will be," Master Cyrus agreed.

"Good. Were you upset after killing Clement Alloway?"

Master Cyrus glanced around the room for a second before looking the sheriff in the eye, "No, sir. I was doing our neighborhood a favor."

"I see," the sheriff said. "And before Clement, you had never killed anyone else?"

"No, sir."

Callum wanted to scream! Did Master Cyrus really expect anybody to believe that? He murdered Clement and felt good about doing so! He had probably convinced himself he was doing his parents or the other slaves a favor by killing all of his family members too! What a sick individual!

"Let's talk about Callum now," the sheriff said.

Callum tensed. Talk about him? Why? Because he had ridden the horse with Clement around the same time he got killed? If the lad wasn't afraid of getting beat to death, he'd have stood and rushed out of the sheriff's office. If he had to sit there, he could only hope the sheriff wouldn't make him stand in front of everybody answering questions like the Gillcrest men were.

"So, Callum was your first slave, right?"

"First and only. Yes, sir," Master Cyrus said.

"Did you like having a slave of your own?"

"Yes, sir."

"What did you like about it?"

Master Cyrus smirked at Callum, "I'm going to get hanged anyway, so I might as well tell it like it is. It was fun striking fear into him. Callum is terrified of me, and I like it that way!"

"Were you ever rougher with him than you should have been?"

"I suppose I could have gone easier on the lad," Master Cyrus said. "But I wasn't abusive or anything. I didn't treat him any harsher than other slaves are treated."

Maybe Callum did want to be questioned! He'd like to tell everybody exactly what Master Cyrus had put him through. What a liar! So far, the sheriff seemed to be doing a good job. Perhaps he would ask Callum, or someone else on the plantation, for the other side of the story.

"Let me see if I understand you correctly, Cyrus. Do you have a fascination with power? With being the one in charge? Do you somehow get a thrill out of having somebody else obey your every command?"

Master Cyrus glanced around the room again. "I had never really thought about it quite that way. But yes, I suppose I do."

"One more thing, Cyrus. Are you the jealous type? In other words, did you ever get jealous when your brothers or sisters got more attention? Or did you ever feel you had a heavier workload than they did?"

"Yes. But that's normal. Everybody gets jealous of their siblings from time to time."

CHAPTER FORTY-ONE

WRAPPING IT UP

The sheriff had Mistress Rosanna change places with Master Cyrus.

"Mistress Rosanna, when I questioned you earlier, several times you were reluctant to answer me."

Mistress Rosanna wiped the tears from her face.

"Why is that?"

"Are you going to hang my baby?"

"I'm the one asking the questions right now, Mistress Rosanna. We will talk about that later.

Why were you so hesitant to give me complete, honest answers?"

"I don't know what you mean, Sheriff."

"Before today, did you know your son took Clement Alloway's life?"

"No, sir. I didn't."

"See, that's an honest answer. Now let me re-ask one from earlier. How many of your children are still alive?"

Mistress Rosanna fanned herself as more tears streamed down her cheeks, "I don't know that I can say."

"That's what I'm talking about, Mistress Rosanna. Why can't you say? We're not leaving here today until you tell me what you know. Those skeletal remains we found on your property... do they belong to your children?"

"I can't do this," Mistress Rosanna insisted. "I just want to go home."

"Mistress Rosanna, did Cyrus take the lives of your other children?"

Mistress Rosanna shook her head, "No, sir. No, he didn't."

"That box I asked your husband and your son about, what do you know about it?"

Mistress Rosanna gasped for breath as she had earlier.

"Calm yourself, Mistress Rosanna. I need you to talk to me. No matter what the truth is, we need to hear it."

"I don't want to get anybody in trouble."

"Somebody has gotten themselves into trouble. And if you don't tell what you know, you're going to join them. You know something about that box. Was it Cyrus or Josiah who put those items there?"

Speechless, Mistress Rosanna looked around the room.

"Talk to me," the sheriff said. "That crate didn't gather your children's possessions on its own, Mistress Rosanna. Who put that collection together?"

Mistress Rosanna closed her eyes and sobbed.

"Ma'am. I need answers. Was it your husband, or was it your son?"

Shaking her head, Mistress Rosanna squeaked, "Neither."

"Come again."

"I... I put them there. I miss my babies." Mistress Rosanna struggled to regain her composure. "No momma wants to lose her babies."

"And no momma should have to," the sheriff agreed. "Other mommas in this community won't be able to sleep comfortably for a long time to come unless whoever is responsible for the deaths of your children is brought to justice. Tell me about that box."

"I..." Mistress Rosanna gasped for air again. "I... had trouble saying goodbye. So, before my children were buried, I'd take something special to them and hide it. Every now and then, when I got to missing them, I'd go out and hold those items in my hands and weep over my babies."

"Before your children were buried? Meaning you're now admitting that besides Cyrus, all of your other children are dead?"

Beads of sweat formed on Mistress Rosanna's forehead. After a brief hesitation, she nodded and whispered a tearful, "Yes."

The room quickly filled with gasps of shock.

"I see," the sheriff said. "So, your children were killed, and before they were buried, you'd hide something that was special to them. Your husband said he didn't see any items in that box belonging to Oliver, yet you said all of your other children are dead. Explain that to me."

"There should be a shepherd's sling in that box," Mistress Rosanna said. "That was Oliver's."

"There's no sling in this box," the sheriff said.

"Well, there was," Mistress Rosanna said. "I placed it there myself. If it's not there, I don't know what happened to it.

Callum glared at Master Cyrus. What kind of monster gives away the only remaining keepsake of his own deceased brother? And for what? To satisfy a gambling debt?

"Let's move on," the sheriff said. "Did you ever tell anybody about this box?"

"No, Sheriff."

"How do you suppose Cyrus knew about it then?" the sheriff asked.

Mistress Rosanna fanned herself. "Not too long ago, I started thinking about how unfair it was that all but one of my children were taken from me. For a short moment, I decided I didn't want to live any longer. Before I had time to act on such a thought, I suddenly realized that box was not providing me the comfort I hoped it would. It was forcing me to hold onto those horrible memories. I was losing my mind. Instead of talking to anybody, I decided it was time to get rid of my collection. I was going to take an ax to it and all its contents. But as I was heading out to the toolshed, I heard somebody coming. I set it down and ran around the corner of the house. I peeked out, hoping I was mistaken, but sure enough, it was

Cyrus. I saw him open the lid and peruse the items. Then he carried the box away. I couldn't say anything. I was afraid to."

"Too afraid? I thought you said Cyrus hadn't killed any of your children?"

"He didn't. I wasn't afraid."

"Did you kill your own offspring then?"

"Of course not! I would never do such a thing!"

"How about your slaves? Did one of them do it?"

"No, Sheriff."

"Was it your husband then?"

Mistress Rosanna raised her eyes toward the ceiling. "Please, please don't make me do this. Josiah, please. Will you speak up?"

"About what?" Master Josiah asked, sounding surprised. "I don't know what you're talking about."

"It was him!" Mistress Rosanna cried out. "My husband killed all of my babies. Cyrus and I have been covering for him all of these years!"

"The woman's out of her mind," Josiah shouted. "I've never killed anybody!"

Callum didn't know what to think anymore. Mistress Rosanna loved her family. He couldn't believe she was accusing her husband of crimes that would guarantee him a death sentence.

Why would she do that? After protecting him for so long? The more Callum thought, the more confident he became. It wasn't Master Josiah. It was Master Cyrus. Mistress Rosanna had lost so many children that the thoughts of burying Master Cyrus drove her to pin the blame on her husband. That had to be it!

"Not true!" Master Cyrus protested. "Father, stop lying to these people. You know what you've done. So do we."

Callum couldn't blame Cyrus for teaming up against his father. One of the Gillcrest men was going to die. Things were about to get ugly.

"What are you saying, son?" Master Josiah asked.

"You have a horrible temper, father! You have been so harsh with what you called discipline that you've been taking out our family one member at a time."

"If you keep lying like that, and we both get out of here alive, I'll show you what discipline is."

Jonah suddenly interrupted, "At the risk of getting lashed for speaking out of turn, I have to speak up. I can't prove it, but I believe Master Josiah killed my son. But that's mere speculation. I personally witnessed the man drown one of his own daughters."

Callum could understand why Mistress Rosanna and Master Cyrus would team up against Master Josiah, but Jonah? Sure, Master Josiah had cruelly whipped him in the past, more than likely for something he didn't even do. But Jonah didn't seem the type to seek revenge.

"I did no—" Master Josiah started to say.

"You were trying to scare her. To show her who was boss. But you held her under too long!"

Master Josiah appeared to be stunned, "You're all crazy. I would never kill anybody, especially not my own children!"

The sheriff punched his desk. "Everybody needs to quiet down. Mistress Rosanna, why did you cover for your husband?"

"Because I love him."

"Because you love him? What about your children? Didn't you say you love them?"

"Yes. Of course, I do!"

"Had you reported your husband the first time he killed one of your children, the rest would still be alive today."

"I didn't kill anybody!" Master Josiah insisted.

"Shut up," the sheriff said. "I've heard enough. Master Josiah Gillcrest has committed multiple murders and will be hanged for his crimes. Master Cyrus Gillcrest has committed one murder, and based on his own testimony, I do not feel the community will be safe as long as he is alive. So, he will be hanged next to his father. Mistress Rosanna, you ought to be ashamed of yourself for what you've allowed to happen in the name of love. You enabled this tragedy. Remember this day for the rest of your life. Never forget the part you played in it. That will be punishment enough. As we wrap this thing up, I would like to thank young Callum McCarthy for having the guts to speak the truth, even when he doubted anyone would listen. If it was not for that young man, Josiah Gillcrest would have continued living as a free man despite his crimes.

CHAPTER FORTY-TWO

JUSTICE IS SERVED

As much as Callum despised Master Cyrus, he didn't want to see him or his father hang.

To say Mistress Rosanna was distraught would have been a significant understatement. As her husband and son were led to their places next to a large oak tree, she fell onto her hands and knees. She was saying something through her sobs that no one could understand through all her blubbering.

Besides Mistress Rosanna, the rest of the crowd stood in complete silence. Callum fought back his emotions, trying to look as unaffected by the events unfolding as possible.

As ropes were placed around the necks of the Gillcrest men, the sheriff said, "Folks, what's about to occur here is nothing short of a tragic necessity. After Reverend Driscoll says a few words, we will proceed with the hanging. Reverend?"

"Good morning, everybody. It's difficult to know what to say under such circumstances. Some folks are here today because they want to see justice served. Others are here to say their final goodbyes or possibly in hopes that somehow these proceedings will not continue. No matter why you're here, we're all about to witness the same event. The sheriff called this a 'tragic necessity,' and that's exactly what it is. In Genesis nine, chapter six, the Bible says, 'Whoso sheddeth man's blood, by man shall his blood be shed: for in the image of God made he man.' Similar passages can be found in the twenty-first chapter of Exodus, the twenty-fourth chapter of Leviticus, and in the thirty-fifth chapter of Numbers. As difficult as it is to put men to death for the crime of murder, it must be done to send a clear message to the rest of us. A message that life is precious and should be preserved at all costs. A message that if you shed another's blood, your blood will be shed. Like you, I hate standing here today. But I would rather these men be hanged than for them to have opportunities to take the lives of anyone else in our community. Let's all bow our heads for a word of prayer.

"Father in Heaven, we humbly come before You this morning as we honor Your Word, to thank You for giving us instructions on how to handle difficult matters like this one. Lord, we ask you to comfort Mr. and Mrs. Alloway as they deal with the unnecessary, unexpected premature death of their son, Clement. We ask you to comfort Mrs. Gillcrest as she witnesses the public execution of both her husband and son. We ask You to give Her the wisdom she will need in the days that lie ahead. Lord, we also ask that you use this scene as a deterrent. That those who witness this scene will never take another man's life into their own hands. We ask these things in Jesus' name. Amen."

Opening his tear-filled eyes, Callum found the Gillcrest men had been placed on horses; the ropes around their necks were stretched tightly across a tree branch and firmly held by several men. Mr. Alloway was standing between the two horses.

"Mr. Alloway," the sheriff said. "The time has come."

Mr. Alloway clapped his hands and hollered, "Get!"

Both horses bolted forward, causing the men to fall and swing from side to side. Callum thought he was going to hurl. Master Josiah appeared to die the moment his body dropped. Master Cyrus, on the other hand, was still alive. With terror-filled eyes and struggling to breathe, he raised his arms and grabbed the rope above his head with both hands. The expression on his face screamed of agony. Callum wanted to close his eyes, but somehow, he couldn't do it. Within minutes, Master Cyrus's face began turning blue. It seemed like an eternity, but eventually he stopped breathing.

It was over. Justice had been served.

Chapter Forty-Three

UNGRATEFULNESS

Mistress Rosanna was feistier than Callum had ever seen her.

"You are a terrible person. Not even a person. You are a horrible, wicked, nasty piece of poor-white earth scratching scum! Because of you, I'm a widow. Because of you, I lost my last child! Now I have to figure out how to run a plantation on my own! I ought to have you beaten within an inch of your life. And I would, but you're not worth it!"

Callum cringed. Mistress Rosanna had always been so kind to him. He hadn't meant to hurt her. At the same time, he didn't feel bad for what he had told the sheriff either. If Mistress

Rosanna ordered one of the other slaves to whip him, he'd have no choice but to accept it. Thankfully, she said he wasn't worth it, so he doubted he had anything to worry about.

"What do you think I'm going to do with you, red-leg?"

"I don't know," Callum replied.

"I do!" Mistress Rosanna shouted. "I'm going to sell you off! And I'm going to pray you'll be bought by a cruel-hearted master who will make you regret the day you wrecked my family! In the meantime, I want you out of my sight. Starting right now, I want you to get out to that field. Don't stop working until it's pitch black out. When you return to your cabin, you can sleep for a few hours. But make sure you're back out in that field before the sun comes up. You better work yourself harder than you have since you've been here because I have absolutely had it with you!"

Callum stood in silence.

"What are you waiting for? Move it!"

"Yes, ma'am," Callum said, deciding he had better not ask her what he was going to do about meals.

Heading to the field, the lad couldn't wrap his head around Mistress Rosanna's sudden change of personality. Shouldn't she appreciate that he had the guts to stop her husband before he wound up killing her too? If Master Josiah had murdered seven of her children, he wouldn't have stopped killing had he not been hanged. Mistress Rosanna should have been grateful.

Hopefully, she would come to her senses before making hasty arrangements to force him off her property. It wasn't that he had ever enjoyed living on the Gillcrest plantation. But with Master Josiah and Master Cyrus both out of the way, things would undoubtedly become much more tolerable than they had been before. Maybe there was a way he could patch things up with her? But what could one do to make up for getting the woman's loved ones executed?

Working harder than he ever had before wasn't going to do the trick. That would simply be following Mistress Rosanna's orders. She wasn't going to allow him enough time to perform any kind deeds for her. It was hopeless! Unless there was a miracle, he would be leaving the Gillcrest plantation. And this time, it wouldn't be of his own free will.

CHAPTER FORTY-FOUR

RUDE AWAKENING

Three men barged through Callum's door. Startled, he jumped up and wiped his eyes. Mistress Rosanna walked in behind the strangers. "Callum," she said, "these men are going to escort you off my property. Give them your full cooperation."

Seeing no way of escape nor any place for negotiations, Callum said, "Yes, ma'am."

"Slide your legs over the side of the bed," one of the men growled, approaching the lad with a pair of shackles in his hand. Callum couldn't stand the thought of wearing those things again, but he knew there was no choice. Gritting his teeth, he extended his legs.

"That's the way, red-leg," the man said before shackling Callum's ankles. "On your feet. Hands in front of you."

Feeling defeated, Callum stood and placed his hands in front of him. The man wrapped a chain around his wrists. "You're doing better than I thought you would, red-leg." He grabbed hold of Callum's right arm, and one of the other men grabbed his left. "Mrs. Gillcrest," the man said, "the timing of your request couldn't have been better. As I told you earlier, there is a slave auction about seven hours from here tomorrow afternoon. Once we fetch a fair price for him, we'll get a payment to you."

"Thank you, gentlemen. And if you have any say-so as to who buys this little piece of filth, please make sure it's someone who won't take anything off of him. We have spoiled this red-leg. He needs to be put in his place."

"Yes, ma'am. We will keep that in mind," one of the men said.

Callum was marched out to a carriage that reminded him of the one he was forced into in Dublin. The only difference was, he knew what was going on this time and wasn't nearly as scared.

When they opened the door to the cart, Callum saw two other slaves, a boy and a girl, both Irish and a little younger than he. "Go to the back," one of the men ordered.

"Yes, sir," Callum said. Thankful he wasn't being manhandled, he moved to the spot where the man was pointing and allowed the fellow to chain him to the other lad in the cart.

"If I were you, red-legs, I'd get some sleep. Tomorrow's going to be a long day."

Go to sleep? On the way to a new, unknown destination? That was highly unlikely.

Callum waited until the cart began driving off before speaking to the others. "Did you both come from the same plantation?" he asked.

The lad didn't answer. The girl said, "No. They picked me up about an hour ago. I don't know how long he's been on here. He hasn't spoken a word."

Callum looked at the lad. He was staring straight in front of him, rarely even blinking. If it wasn't for his chest moving up and down, he would have looked dead.

"Why are they selling you?" Callum asked the girl.

"My mistress fell on hard times and couldn't afford me anymore."

"They kept all their other slaves and only sold you?"

"I was the youngest," she replied. "They said I wasn't able to do as much work as the others, and they had to get rid of somebody. What about you? Why are you being sold?"

"I don't feel like talking about it right now."

"Oh," the girl said.

The boy suddenly turned and gave Callum a dirty look. "You asked her why she was being sold, and she answered. Now you be polite enough to answer her."

"So, he can speak," Callum said.

"Answer her," the lad demanded. "Now!"

"And what if I don't?"

"Do it!"

Callum smirked, "Okay, I'll humor you. I caused some problems for the plantation owner."

"Some problems? That's not an answer," the lad said. "What kind of problems?"

Callum shook his head. "It's a long story, but I found out the planter had murdered seven of his children, and I got word of it to the sheriff. They hanged him."

"You're lying."

"No, I'm not," Callum replied. "So, how did you wind up here?"

"Rebelled one time too many, I guess. My master said I was too much trouble."

"You made me elaborate," Callum said. "Your turn. What did you do to rebel?"

"It's more like what did I not do?" the lad laughed. "I refused to acknowledge the new name they gave me, no matter how many times they beat me. I wouldn't call the planter sir or his wife ma'am. I stole the master's whip and threw it in a creek. I think what really did it was when I kissed the master's daughter."

Callum laughed, "You really did all of that?"

"And then some."

The girl said, "No wonder they're selling you off. Aren't you afraid of how they might treat you at the next plantation?"

"Men aren't afraid of anything or anybody," the lad replied.

For the next few hours, Callum passed the time by getting better acquainted with the two other slaves he shared the cart with before eventually falling into a deep sleep.

He didn't wake up until the cart came to a halt, and the door to his carriage was whisked open. Within what felt like only seconds, he and the other two slaves were taken out of the cart and ordered to join the ranks of many other slaves up for bid.

Callum looked at the lineup. Out of fifteen slaves, all but three were Irish. At a steady pace, he approached and stood next to the last slave in line.

Not quite as uneasy as he had been during the first auction, Callum turned this one into a mental game. As the crowd gathered in front of him, he examined the expressions on their faces. Who would he most likely go home with, and how might they treat him? What would their plantation be like? And how high of a bid would be offered for him?

"Alright, folks," the auctioneer spoke loudly, "At this time, we're going to allow you to examine the prospects. The auction will begin approximately three hours from now."

This was the part of the auction Callum had dreaded the most. The part where he would be treated like a piece of meat.

A young man close to Master Cyrus's age stepped up in front of him. "This guy looks like he knows how to work," he said, feeling Callum's shoulders. "What's your name?"

"Callum."

"Callum, huh? Interesting name." The fellow walked around behind him. "Looks like you've had a whip taken to you a time or two. Hopefully, that means somebody drove some of that red-leg rebellion out of you."

The fellow walked around to the front of him again and stared him in the eye. "I'm not so sure about that. You look like the kind that would give a man trouble. I don't know."

Callum hoped that man would lose interest in him. His age reminded him too much of Master Cyrus. He would probably fare better under the hand of someone older. Someone more experienced. Someone a little less power hungry, perhaps.

An older woman approached him, "Definitely not this one," she said to herself. "He's strong enough. But there's something about those eyes."

Immediately following her came a man who made Callum cringe. He was a middle-aged fellow who carried himself as if he owned the world. The look he gave Callum said, "You're going to be mine. Nobody can outbid me."

Callum didn't want to go home with him. He looked like he was capable of inflicting brutal punishments for the most minor of offenses. A man who could most likely use his money to get away with any crime he chose to commit. The potential buyer looked Callum in the eye for a second. "Lower your eyes, cracker. You are not my equal."

Callum despised that man but complied with the order. The fellow chuckled. "You obeyed on the outside, but on the inside, you were screaming, 'If you buy me, I'll make you wish you hadn't.' Ha. I love breaking the wills of young crackers like you. I'd welcome the challenge."

The man circled him, felt his arms, looked at the bottoms of his feet, and examined his teeth. "I think this one might do quite nicely," he said before finally moving on.

As the potential buyer walked away, something struck Callum. That last man seemed oddly familiar. His voice, his nose, those piercing eyes. But who could he be? It wasn't like Callum knew anyone in the colonies.

A younger married couple approached. "What do you think of this one?" the man asked.

"He's okay," his wife said. "Strong arms. Could be easy to manage. Your thoughts?"

The man pushed his spectacles up on his nose. "He's a hard one to read. A part of me thinks he would be a fast learner, a hard worker, and a good servant all the way around. Another part of me thinks he would require a lot of supervision, plenty of lashings, and wouldn't be worth the investment."

Callum wasn't sure he wanted to go home with any of these folks. What he wanted was to return to Dublin. Or if he had to be auctioned off, he wanted it to be done and over with. This inspection process was far too unnerving.

Callum couldn't get his mind off the fierce middle-aged fellow who had so incredibly intimidated him. He wasn't crazy. He had crossed paths with that man somewhere in his past.

Three hours felt like an eternity. But eventually, the auction began.

"We're going to open up the auction with bids for this sixteen-year-old maidservant." Scared out of his mind, Callum's eyes moved from the auctioneer to the girl he was selling off. "Whether you want her to work the fields, serve in the kitchen, or birth more slaves, this girl will be well worth your investment. Who will bid ten shillings?"

Callum watched with anticipation as person after person placed their offer, and the young lady was awarded to the highest bidder.

"Next, we have a lad of only six years old. He'll probably go cheap as he has much training ahead of him and won't yet be able to perform much heavy lifting. But invest in the lad now, and you'll have a workhorse later on. Will anyone bid two shillings?"

Six years old? Callum couldn't help but wonder where the lad's family was. Or what kind of a future that child might have. He hoped the little one would be sold to a kind master. To someone who might treat him more like a son than a slave.

Scanning the crowd, Callum saw him. That man who said he loved the challenge of breaking the wills of young crackers. The fellow made eye contact with Callum. The lad quickly diverted his eyes. If he were to be bid on, he sure hoped that man wasn't interested.

Wait a minute! No, it couldn't be. Uncle Keir was back at home, trying to defend the people of Dublin from slavers. That couldn't be him. There was no way he was in the colonies. And even if he was, the last thing he'd involve himself in was owning other human beings, especially others who were Irish.

Callum wanted to take another look at the will-breaker but was terrified of making eye contact again. He didn't want to give anyone ideas. And something about that man, even though he looked like his uncle, was spooky. Callum wanted nothing to do with him.

"Look at this twenty-one-year-old male," the auctioneer said. "This young lad is strong and healthy. He's good-looking and well-mannered. He's a bargain at any price. Who'll bid twenty shillings?"

One after another, Callum watched slaves being auctioned off. Finally, it was his turn. "Last but certainly not least, we have a strong, handsome thirteen-year-old lad here. He'll make a nice addition to any plantation. Who will start the bidding at fifteen shillings?"

Callum could no longer pretend this was a game. No longer could he make light guesses about who would bid the highest for him. It was the moment of truth — the moment when his future would be decided.

As long as he didn't go home with that man who reminded him of Uncle Keir, the fellow who was now staring at him with a wicked grin on his face, he would be okay.

"I'll bid ten shillings," a lady called out.

"I'll give eleven," Uncle Keir's look-alike said.

Callum struggled to breathe. Closing his eyes, he wished this day could be over. Not that he was offered any hope of having a better tomorrow.

"Twelve," the intimidating will-breaker shouted.

A NOTE FROM THE AUTHOR

Thank you for reading the first book in the white slave series! As an independently published author, I heavily rely on word-of-mouth advertising and reviews to keep my books in front of as many potential readers as possible. It would be a huge help if you would tell your social media and/or book club friends about *Brutalized* as well as if you would write a three or four sentence review online.

INFURIATED

Don't forget to order *Infuriated*, the second book in the white slave series to see how Callum fares under his new master.

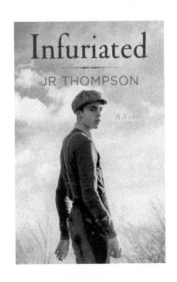

OTHER BOOKS BY JR THOMPSON

The Worthy Battle Series
Rebuilding Alden
Redirecting Billy
Reprogramming Carlos
Reforming Dawson
Renovating Elliot
Refurbishing Felipe

The Harmony Series
Hidden in Harmony
Fighting for Farmington
Terrors of Troy
Storms at Shelton